THE
POSTWOMAN

MICHAEL KENNETH SMITH

BASED ON THE TRUE STORY OF ANDRÉE DE JONGH

ISBN: 1979092036
ISBN 13: 9781979092036
Library of Congress Control Number: 2017916643
CreateSpace Independent Publishing Platform
North Charleston, South Carolina

CODE POEM FOR THE FRENCH RESISTANCE

The life that I have
Is all that I have
And the life that I have is yours.

The love that I have
Of the life that I have,
Is yours and yours and yours.

A sleep I shall have,
A rest I shall have,
Yet death will be but a pause.

For the peace of my years
In the long green grass,
Will be yours and yours and yours.

by Leo Marks

Chapter 1

JUNE 1940

The young English soldier's face lit up when Dedee approached his bed. His shrapnel-lacerated arm had mostly healed, and he was due to be released soon. She frowned, and put her finger to her pursed lips. The door to the fifty-bed ward burst open and two German SS officers entered. Dedee quickly dabbed a yellowish red fluid on the Englishman's bandages. The smell was disgusting.

The two Germans were doing their weekly inspection of the soldiers, most of whom had been injured in the recent fighting near Dunkirk. When released from the hospital, the English soldiers would be shipped to workcamps in Germany. The SS officers stopped at each bed and asked to see the patient's wounds. If they thought the wounds were healed, they marked their chart, and the patient would be shipped out the next day. When the SS officers approached the bed by which Dedee stood, they didn't even ask to see the wound. Wrinkling their noses at the smell, they quickly moved on.

Dedee winked at the Englishman and left the ward. She thought back to when she was a little girl and a neighbor boy would always take her bicycle without her permission. She'd smeared Limburger cheese on the handlebars, and it never happened again. Rumors were the workcamps were more like death camps. The Germans were using the labor of English soldiers to bolster the Weimar's war effort. Dedee found that idea abhorrent.

Later, on the way home to her flat, she passed the home of one of the attending Belgian doctors, a longtime friend of her father's. She knew him to be an excellent doctor, but also a passionate patriot who despised the Germans almost as much as she did. She knocked on his door. She was thinking there had to be a way to help the British soldiers, or at least keep them from being sent to labor camps. The doctor answered and immediately let her in.

"Quite a stunt you pulled today," he said with a smile. "We still haven't got that smell out of the ward. I can still smell it on my clothing." He offered tea, which she accepted. They sat in his kitchen in awkward silence.

The doctor knew Dedee well enough to know her visit was not a social call. "I think that poor soldier would've been shipped out tomorrow if you hadn't saved the day," he said, trying to get a conversation started.

"Do the other doctors feel the way you do, Doctor?" She asked.

"Almost all. But we can't keep the patients in the hospital forever," he said. "Maybe we could hide them somewhere."

"Yes, but where?" she asked. "There would be hundreds. Maybe thousands."

"Anyplace big enough for that would be discovered," he said.

"We have an extra bedroom at my parent's place. We could handle one or two," she said.

"My wife and I do, also—but the risk is huge. The consequence of getting caught would be prison…or worse."

Dedee hardly noticed the rain as she walked back to her father's apartment in the Schaerbeek District. She traveled this route twice a day, and despite the discomfort caused by her wet clothing, her mind reeled. A trained commercial artist, Andrée

(Dedee) de Jongh was a petite young woman, standing five feet two inches tall. She was svelte, and attractive. Her short brown hair was naturally curly, and her blue eyes flared with intensity, intelligence, and determination. When the Belgian hospitals had started filling up with British wounded during the Dunkirk debacle, she'd volunteered as a nurse, and was appalled by the huge number of British soldiers who filled their hospitals. Both Dedee and her father were sickened by how quickly their country had succumbed to the German blitz and what many considered a premature Belgian surrender by King Leopold III to Nazi Germany. Dedee frequently wrote letters to the parents or families of her patients, notifying them that their son or husband was alive. She hated the Germans, and it was that hatred that would keep her focused through the troubling times ahead.

As she turned a corner and started the slow uphill grade to her house, she noticed a Kübelwagen parked on the opposite side of the street. The engine was running and both windshield wipers were on high and out of sync. Blue smoke came out of the exhaust, and rain drops spat and steamed when they hit the hot pipe. Both doors were open, and Dedee could see no one in the vehicle, but she heard voices. Then she heard a man screaming.

As she crossed the street for a better view, Dedee saw two German soldiers beating an older man. One was hitting the man with a schlagstock and the other was kicking him with his boot. The man, who was trying to protect himself with his hands and arms, had a star sewn onto his jacket.

One of the Germans kept yelling, "Verdammter Jude!" *Damned Jew!* over and over.

Dedee approached the Kübelwagen from the opposite side and reached in through the open door and released the center-mounted parking brake. The vehicle started to coast backwards, gradually picking up speed.

Dedee screamed, and the two soldiers looked up and immediately bolted after their truck, leaving the old man alone, struggling to stand.

When Dedee approached the man, he stood unsteadily.

With her arm around him in support, she whispered, "Is your home nearby?"

When he said it was just around the corner, she helped him to his door and wished him good luck.

He unlocked the door, and taking both her hands in his, said, "Toda raba," *Thank you very much.*

Only after she arrived at her father's house did Dedee realize she was soaking wet.

The gentle rain that had been falling when she started had turned into a downpour, and she had hardly noticed. She changed out of her wet clothes and put on her robe, wrapped her hair in a towel, and began fixing dinner for herself and her father.

She was comfortable in the kitchen. Moving efficiently, she prepared a fish stew that her mother often served when it was cold and rainy. Food supplies had already become scarce as German officials confiscated much of what was available, to be shipped back to Germany. Dedee was thankful that her mother had wisely stocked up on canned goods, anticipating shortages.

Her mother was attending her sick sister in Ghent, about fifty miles north, and they did not know how soon she could return.

Her father, Paul, arrived through the back door and called a greeting. She could hear him removing his rain slicker and hanging his umbrella to dry.

Dedee smiled, thinking her father at least had enough sense to stay dry in the rain. He was fifty-eight years old, wore thick spectacles, and his gray hair was combed back, creating a scholarly look worthy of his teaching profession. In addition to being an administrator at a boys school, he taught physics to the seniors, and when Dedee was younger, they spent hours talking about how and why mechanical things worked the way they did. The two of them also agreed on almost all things political: a strong government, good education, social programs for the poor and underprivileged, and most of all, women's rights.

Paul could see that Dedee was excited about something. He asked, "How was your day?"

She told him about the run-in with the two German soldiers at the hospital and laughed when she described the way they had hastily left when they smelled the pongy fluid taken from a man who had drowned.

Then she related the incident with the drunks in the Kübelwagen. Paul said he had heard of several other such incidences. He related how the Germans occupied Belgium in The Big War, friendly at first, then increasingly aggressive, especially with women. They both knew their behavior would only get worse... A lot worse.

"Paul, I stopped by the flat of one of our staff doctors today on the way home," Dedee said. Since early childhood, Dedee had called her father by his first name. Paul had insisted on it. It was a tradition in his family, and Paul thought it brought everyone to the same level, for easier conversation. She called him 'father' only when she wanted to express her love for him.

Paul knew Dedee was finally getting to what she really wanted to say, and what she was so excited about. "And?" he asked.

She smiled. "We can't let these wounded British soldiers go to German workcamps," she said. "All that accomplishes is the Germans get stronger and we get weaker. We not only have soldiers wounded from Dunkirk, but we also have RAF fliers who have been shot down."

"This is true, but what do we do? Hide them?"

Dedee was silent. Then she said, "We could ship them back to England...?" It was almost like a question.

"How? Surely the channel is well patrolled," Paul said.

"Maybe we escort them into Spain."

"Franco wouldn't like that," Paul said, "but their chances would be better in Spain than in Belgium...or France."

Dedee served dinner, and the two of them continued their discussion for several hours.

Long before dawn, the smell of fresh coffee woke Paul and he walked into the kitchen to see Dedee sitting at the table writing on a tablet. She had a pile of notes stacked up in front of her.

"You been here all night?" he asked.

"Paul, I've got it. I think we can do it," she said.

He poured himself a cup of coffee and sat next to his daughter. He always knew when she was excited because the veins on each side of her forehead stood out.

She started to read her notes. "We're going to escort them over the Pyrenees. We'll need safe houses. Lots of them. All along the way. Then we need guides to take them from one safe house to another. We need travel documents. Good ones. We will need coordinators to handle small details. Mountain guides. Most of all, we'll need money for food, train tickets, and the forgeries."

Paul frowned. "A bullet through the head if you're caught. Or even worse, torture."

She pretended she didn't hear him. "A friend of mine has a close and willing friend in Anglet, near the Spanish border and…"

"You mean to cross the Pyrenees? What then?" Paul asked.

"San Sebastián, Bilbao, then Gibraltar. The flyers can just get in another airplane and continue to fight," she said flatly.

Paul thought a moment, then smiled. "Still in love with anybody who flies an airplane, aren't you?"

Dedee blushed. "Not true. I'd kill a Luftwaffe pilot without even thinking about it."

Paul studied his daughter from across the table. She was twenty-four years old, soon to be twenty-five. He thought she had the best traits of her mother—especially her determination. He had hoped she would find a good husband and settle down to raise a family, but when the Germans outsmarted the English again at Dunkirk, using the same trick they had pulled in the Big War, she had immediately volunteered as a nurse's aide, to care for the wounded.

Paul remembered how, at the age of five, Dedee would sit on his lap and beg for him to tell her stories about Jean Mermoz, the famous French fighter pilot who had made himself a hero in Syria when France and Belgium sorely needed heroes after the Great War. She never tired of it. She learned to recognize the various patches on soldiers' uniforms that signified they were part of an aviation crew, and whenever she saw one, she would try to shake the soldier's hand.

"Seems like money may be the biggest obstacle," Paul said, taking Dedee's plan seriously.

"I've got that figured too, Paul," she said.

"I think I'm afraid to ask," he said.

She waited to let the drama build. "The British will pay," she announced.

"The British?"

"Of course. Think of it. Who will benefit by the return of their fliers? They must spend thousands on training, and for each one we return, they will save thousands."

Paul poured another cup of coffee and sat down again. "You just might be right," he said. "But, if they finance the operation, they're going to want to control it. If they control it, we might have difficulty keeping everything secret."

"I was thinking about that also. I think they will want their fliers back a lot more than they will want control. Especially if we insist that we remain autonomous."

Over the next several weeks, they made lists of friends and acquaintances who might be willing to help. In addition, and equally important, they made another coded list of friends who might be willing to contribute money. Paul had some meager savings, and they agreed much, much more was required. But even if all their friends were extremely generous, the funds would not be nearly enough. As each day passed, their enthusiasm and commitment increased.

Chapter 2

❦

AUGUST 1940

Dedee eyed the plump British woman sitting across from her. She had been told her name was Miss Richards. On her head was a large Panama hat, and beside her was a huge suitcase. Miss Richards wore a white dress trimmed in pink lace, hardly the proper attire for crossing the Pyrenees. She was supposedly wanted by the Gestapo, but Dedee was never able to verify that information. In addition to the woman, ten Belgian men, also wanted by the Gestapo, were in her charge. The train they were on rambled toward Quievrain, on the French/Belgian border. They would get off at the border, go through French customs, and board another train to La Corbie, near Amiens, then cross the Somme on foot.

The woman and the ten men were Dedee's first attempt at escorting fugitives to the Pyrenees and hopefully through Spain and down to Gibraltar. During the last few weeks, she had spent all her free time developing contacts and resources. Dedee, with eager assistance from her father, had decided that their little operation had to be controlled from three different locations: Brussels, Paris, and a base on the east side of the Pyrenees.

The Brussels base would gather the British soldiers and downed RAF flyers and get them into France. Dedee's father would be in charge and their duties would also be to discreetly spread the word through the Belgian Resistance that downed flyers were valuable and an organization existed that could help them get back to England. The job was huge because the flyers might be forced down anywhere in Belgium, and those farmers and property owners who first encountered them would have to hide, feed, and re-clothe them while they waited for the organization to arrange to move them toward France.

The Paris base was charged with getting the evaders through France and down to the Pyrenees safely. This would require new sets of travel documents, more safe houses, and guides to take them from one safe house to another.

Finally, the base near the mountains would arrange for guides to get the soldiers over the mountains and into Spain. That part of the journey was particularly difficult because the evaders would need special clothing to climb, and because of frequently inclement weather, they would have to be housed until favorable conditions prevailed.

When she had contacted the Belgian Underground, they were not sure they could trust her, but their doubts were assuaged by her eagerness and obvious hatred of the German occupiers. When she explained to them that she was attempting to set up an organization to escort evaders into Spain, they reluctantly agreed to give her a try. This group of eleven did not fit her idea of transporting RAF fliers, but they wanted to escape occupied Europe, and Dedee knew she needed experience before she tried genuine RAF evaders, so she reluctantly agreed to escort them.

The Belgian Resistance was not yet well organized, and Dedee was told the ten men were being held at three different safe houses, and the woman in another. They would all have papers. Armed with the four addresses, she had proceeded on foot and picked them all up and escorted them to the Brussels train station. The men looked more like field hands, dressed in farmer's clothing and knee boots covered in cow dung. She assumed these men probably wanted to get into the war even more than they feared the Gestapo. That was fine with her because all she wanted to do was prove to the Resistance that she was capable.

With the assistance of Arnold de Pe, a Belgian Resistance member and friend of Paul's, they had split the group in two: Arnold with five Belgians, and Dedee with the other five and the woman. Their papers were hand forged, and Dedee was nervous. She sat, quietly looking out the window as the train passed through the Belgian countryside. Her mind was on the task ahead and all the things that might go wrong. An agent might question their papers. A German officer might stop them for questioning. Were the safe houses safe? She analyzed every possibility and tried to make a plan for each. She was excited. This was her first trip. She would turn the entire group over to a mountain guide who would escort them over the mountains, then return to Brussels for her first attempt with real soldiers, whom she would accompany over the Pyrenees to the British consulate.

The conductor came down the aisle, announcing that they were approaching Corbie. Dedee stood, as did the five Belgians in her charge. Miss Richards stood, picked up her umbrella, and stared at Dedee. She looked at her heavy bag then back to Dedee. Disgusted, Dedee, picked up the bag and dragged it to the door. She thought to herself that the woman might be big trouble.

They stopped at a café for supper, and the hot July air was replaced by a cool evening breeze.

The café was not crowded. Dedee's group ate quickly, and Arnold led them down to the river in the darkness. The Somme flowed quietly, its shallow banks muddy from recent rains. They rounded a bend and neared the copse where Arnold had had his contact Nennette hide the small boat that would take them across. Nennette was to meet them after they crossed. They heard a noise ahead, and when Arnold suddenly stopped, the whole group ran into each other, and the woman fell in the mud.

Dedee knew the woman was about to scream, so she reached down and put her hand over her mouth, just in time.

Arnold went to investigate, and when he returned, he whispered that a group of campers were just ahead and they would not be able to use the hidden boat because it was too near the campsite. Everyone looked to Dedee for guidance.

After hesitating a moment to collect her thoughts, she took a deep breath, and said, "We're going to swim across. The river is not very deep and the current is mild. We'll go one at a time. How many can swim?"

When only six of the Belgians indicated they could, she silently cursed her bad luck. "Okay, Arnold, we'll need a long cable to string across the river. And a tire tube for those that can't swim. Please see if you can find these things at the farm we passed earlier."

Arnold got up promptly and left.

"I can't do it," Miss Richards said. "I can't swim. And I will not get wet trying to float in an inner tube." She held her chin up defiantly.

Dedee looked at her squarely. "You can and you will," she said with confident authority. "Please, everyone, get some rest until Arnold returns."

Dedee saw a light approaching on the pathway beside the river. She whispered for everyone to get down and lie as flat as possible. It was a bicycle headlight, and as the rider passed, she could see the outline of a German helmet, and a rifle strapped to the soldier's back. Dedee cursed under her breath. Something else she hadn't planned and was unprepared for.

Arnold returned an hour later. The farmer had been friendly, and had gave him exactly what they needed: a long rope and an inflated inner tube from a tractor tire. He tied one end of the rope to a nearby tree, then slipped into the water, slowly uncoiling the rope as he swam to the other side. When he had secured the other end to a tree, he jerked on the rope, which was Dedee's signal to start bringing the others across. The six Belgians who could swim, took their outer clothing off and swam across, dragging a log with their clothes tied to it. They were met by Arnold's contact Nennette, who would escort the group to her farmhouse nearby.

Dedee helped the first non-swimming Belgian. She slipped into the water and her feet sank into the mud. She could feel the mud ooze between her toes. The water was surprisingly cold. He was a big young man, and obviously very uncomfortable in the water, which was made worse by the water's shocking chill. When he was finally able to ensconce himself in the tire, he clearly seemed too nervous to pull himself across, so Dedee, who had already shed her shoes and socks, took off her white blouse and plaid skirt and propelled him easily across using a sidestroke. She returned for the next passenger and repeated the process until all were across but one, Miss Richards.

Dedee told the woman to take her clothes off, so she would have something dry to put on after she crossed. The woman refused. Dedee insisted. The two women glared at each other, but Dedee held firm and Miss Richards was the first to blink. Dedee deposited the woman's dry clothes in a basket, which was placed on a log along with some of other items she had taken from the woman's oversized bag. Miss Richards was angry, and her whispers rose in pitch and tenor. Dedee was afraid she would be heard, so she again placed her hand over the woman's mouth. Finally, Dedee squeezed Miss Richards' derriere into the center of the inner tube and started to push her across the river. The inner tube, which had evidently come from a tractor tire, was almost completely submerged beneath the woman. As Dedee pushed from the rear, it tilted forward, and the woman pitched into the water, almost head first. The tube, when relieved of the weight, popped into the air and landed downstream. Dedee had to hold the woman up so she wouldn't drown. She told the woman to try to relax in the water and not fight it, but her pleas were not heard as the panicked woman thrashed. Dedee saw another light on the path, approaching from upriver. The rider would almost certainly hear the splashing. In an instant, Dedee swung her fist, landing a direct blow on the side of Miss Richards' head. The thrashing stopped, and the woman became inert in the water, sinking below the surface. Dedee took a deep breath and went down after her. She grabbed her hair, pulled her to the surface, and silently sidestroked to the other side, as the bicyclist's light disappeared around the bend.

Arnold helped pull the woman onto the riverbank, and she slowly regained consciousness, spitting out water. Dedee, who had been in the river for almost an hour, sat down, trying to stop shivering. She was cold and exhausted. She rubbed her legs briskly to get the blood flowing, and slowly, she could feel goosebumps disappear. She put her dry skirt and blouse back on and the three of them walked up to Nennette's farmhouse.

Even though all eleven had eventually crossed safely, she knew they could not afford to make the same mistakes again. She had failed to anticipate the possibility of a German patrol and the problems with Miss Richards, both of which could have spelled disaster.

⚞⚟

Days later, Dedee headed back to Brussels. She and Arnold had delivered the ragtag group to a contact Arnold had previously established in Anglet, at the foot of the Pyrenees. From there, a guide would escort them across the treacherous passes into Spain, and then on to Gibraltar.

Adjusting to the rhythmic swaying of the train car, Dedee made coded notes. There were so many things that needed to be done and she would have to rely on her father to help. The forged papers had to be better than the ones they had used with the Belgians. They had to be professional. She didn't care for the guide they had used to take the evaders over the mountains. The man, known only as Thomas, acted like he would do anything for money, and his lack of enthusiasm for the Allied cause gave her some trepidation. Then, there continued to be the problem of money. It always came down to money, and she wanted the British to pay. It would be tricky, she knew, but she was bolstered by her initial success and confident in her ability to get it done.

When she arrived back in Brussels, Paul was ready. He had two Belgians who wanted to go to England and join the war against Germany, and one Scottish soldier who had survived St. Valery. They were in three different safe houses in the Brussels area, and Paul informed her he had papers for all three, then he proudly gave them to her.

"Paul, these are excellent," she said. "How much did you have to pay?"

"We aren't the only ones in Brussels who hate the Germans," he said. "Those were made by a jeweler."

Dedee smiled at her father. Normally he would tell her the name of such a person, but they both realized that she had no need to know, and the fewer who knew these things, the better. A siren could be heard in the distance. "Paul," she said, "we're going to make this happen."

Chapter 3

❦

SEPTEMBER 1940

The two Belgians were seated together two rows behind her, and the Scottish soldier sat next to her in an aisle seat, on the train headed to Bayonne. The soldier, whose name was Ian, wore peasant clothing topped off by an old green woolen beret. His papers said he was twenty, and the smile never left his face. He was always talking, and Dedee had to repeatedly hush him, as his Scottish brogue was a dead giveaway. He had a round face, red hair, and intense blue eyes. Dedee found him attractive, but she was worried how he would react if questioned by the German police. She had told him to keep a copy of *Le Monde* in front of him to discourage others from talking to him. She worried less about the Belgians. She knew they could handle themselves because they spoke French.

They had left Brussels four days before, and their crossing at Le Corbie had been uneventful. Nennette had moved the little boat downstream and away from the camping area. All four had crossed at the same time. Thomas would guide them over the Pyrenees, and she planned to take them personally all the way to the British Consulate in Bilbao. She had just enough money to pay for Thomas, meals, and train tickets. She prayed the Brits would help her.

On the last stop before Anglet, two SS soldiers boarded and sat next to Ian in the two seats across the aisle. Before they sat down, both glanced at him, but their eyes locked on Dedee, and they immediately took off their visor caps, placed them under their arms, and bowed, lightly clicking their heels together in near unison. Dedee stared at the silver Totenkopf skull and crossbones pins just below their swastikas and she felt the hatred she had harbored since the German blitz of her homeland. She held the Germans' gaze, but did not acknowledge them. They seemed to be on leave. Both were laughing, enjoying each other's company. The train moved off, and they started to talk in French, as if they wanted everyone on board to join in their revelry.

The one closest to Ian told a story about a Russian woman. He laughed heartily at his own joke and slapped Ian on the shoulder as if he should enjoy the joke also. Ian kept his nose in his paper, and the German stopped laughing. Only the ratta-tat, ratta-tat of the car's wheels could be heard. The German soldier's broad grin turned to a frown as he glared at the Scotsman. Ian hadn't understood a word they'd said. The paper crinkled in his clenched hands. Ratta-tat, ratta-tat.

Dedee glanced at the closest soldier's sidearm. It was a regular issue Lugar. A symbol of the repression of freedom-loving peoples by this fanatical regime bent on world domination. She saw that both wore wedding rings. She could smell one of the soldiers' cologne. It had an arrogance to it, a kind of attitude of *I'm better than you*. It also hinted that the soldier was willing to cheat on his wife. Dedee felt a coolness sweep over her. One that would come over her again and again in the next few months. It was like putting a pair of new glasses on and everything coming into sharp focus.

She put her hand on Ian's left thigh and leaned against him suggestively. In a soft voice, she told the soldiers they were going to St. Jean de Luc to get married. The Germans looked doubtful and stared at Dedee's hand, which was moving erotically up and down Ian's inner thigh. Ian didn't know what Dedee had told them, but he got the gist of it. He put his paper down and leaned over and kissed her. Any doubt the two Germans still had faded away as the kiss lingered. Dedee wrapped her arms around him and held him close. She kept her eyes shut so the soldiers wouldn't think she was faking. She could smell and taste the Scotsman, and she liked it. Finally, when the conductor came through, announcing 'Anglet,' they separated. Dedee had to look out the window to hide her amusement as the two German soldiers relaxed and continued their chatter. She felt like she had just won a game of chess, and the taste of her little victory was sweet. The others in the train car resumed conversation, but most kept their eyes on the Germans.

Ian and Dedee got up to leave. The two Germans both said, "Die beaten Wunche," *best wishes,* and laughed. Then one said, "koch bin kuss?" *one more kiss?* Dedee quickly gave Ian a peck on the cheek, then, just before they stepped off the car, Ian looked back at the Germans and winked and moved his hips forward and back. The Germans roared.

Still holding Ian's hand, out of sight of the departing train, Dedee asked, "What did you do?"

"I winked at them," he said.

"Don't you ever take a chance like that again," Dedee said.

He pulled on her hand to stop her. The breeze blew her hair. He looked her in the eyes. "Did you mean it?" he asked.

She looked at him for a second, then said, "Of course not."

With the two Belgians following twenty paces behind, Dedee led them to the small gray villa she had taken the others to just five weeks before. The back of the villa overlooked the bay of St. Jean de Luc, and had a beautiful view of the mountains from the front. The stones of the driveway crunched with each step. She could smell the bay, and when she stepped up on the porch, she could see it through the house. She knocked on the door softly. This was the home of Elvire de Greef, a contact Arnold had found earlier in the year. A dog barked, and Dedee could hear soft footsteps approaching from within. The door opened and Elvire's dog, Gogo, rushed out to greet her, remembering her from her from her previous visit. Elvire was one of those rare people who commanded attention. She was Dedee's height, with short dark hair. Her brown eyes exhibited deep intelligence and gave her a countenance of always knowing and understanding what was happening. She and her husband, Fernand, were from Belgium, and had moved to Anglet to get away from the Germans. They had intended to move farther into Spain, but this is where they'd ended up.

While the two Belgians and the Scotsman were having sandwiches, Dedee and Elvire walked out onto the lawn overlooking the bay. In the late afternoon sun, they sat on two beach chairs. They were safely out of earshot.

"I'm sorry to tell you some bad news," Elvire said. "When Thomas, our guide, entered Spain with the ten Belgians and Miss Richards, they were immediately arrested by the Carabinaros. Fortunately, Thomas got away."

Dedee was silent, letting the news sink in. "Were they tipped off?"

"I only know what Thomas told me. They are probably in the concentration camp in Miranda," Elvire said.

Dedee slapped the palm of her hand on the arm of the chair. "This is ridiculous. What good is it if we hide and feed people who want to escape, then get them over the Pyrenees only to be captured and put away? This cannot happen."

"What shall we do?" Elvire asked.

Dedee thought for a moment. "The British will have to meet them and take them to Gibraltar. They can use their diplomatic immunity."

"Not sure their 'diplomatic immunity' is any good anymore," Elvire said.

"We'll see about that," Dedee said, and stood to go back into the house.

"How are you going to get across the mountain passes?" Elvire asked.

"Thomas."

"He won't take you. The long trek over is steep and treacherous and he thinks only men are strong enough to cross."

"We'll see about that," Dedee said. She smiled and added,
"Also."

The next morning, before sunup, Elvire prepared a huge
breakfast including eggs, ham, pastries, and lots of hot coffee.
Ian nervously jabbered to the Belgians, who just nodded at everything he said because they didn't understand English. When
he laughed, they laughed, which made him talk even more.

When they were finished, they all went out on the front porch
and Thomas told the three of them what to expect. He empha-
sized the difficulty and reminded them that only the strongest
could make the crossing. He seemed pleased that the three men
looked in reasonable condition.

Elvire came out with five backpacks loaded with food and
rain gear.

Thomas looked at the packs. "Why five? There are only four
of us."

Dedee picked up a pack, slung it over her shoulder, and announced she was going.

Thomas said, "Oh no you're not." He looked her up and down
and smiled mockingly. "You couldn't make it up the first of the
foothills. You're too frail."

Dedee approached him. "You're wrong. Give me a chance. If
at any time I fall behind, I'll agree to turn around and come back.
But there's no chance of that."

Privately, Dedee didn't care much for Thomas. His ingrained
misogyny only deepened her dislike for him. They needed another guide.

The sky was cloudy and the temperature unusually warm
when they departed. The first several miles would be by bicycle,
following little-used roads that led to the actual foothills. Thomas

instructed them to each stay within sight of the next, but keeping a good distance between them. She looked ahead at the mountains, their tops obscured by clouds. She knew the next forty-eight hours were critical to the success of her plans. She had to deliver her 'packages' all the way to the consulate in Bilbao. She had tried to think of everything that could go wrong and knew only success was just over the perilous mountains ahead.

The little road they were traveling came to an end with several paths leading off in different directions. They hid their bikes in a nearby copse where Elvire's daughter Janine would pick them up later. Thomas started out at a brisk pace. He told Dedee to follow him, then the Scotsman and the two Belgians. The trail grew gradually steeper and Thomas seemed to increase the pace. He was dark haired, about thirty-five, and had spent all his years in the mountains. His father had been a smuggler, as had been his grandfather, and most thought that Thomas was a smuggler also,

Dedee could hear the men behind her breathing hard. As the climb became more difficult, Dedee got closer to Thomas, so that every time he looked around, she was right there with him, step-for-step. Dedee had always loved to exercise. Before the war, she swam nearly every day with her father, who had always been impressed by her speed and endurance. The trail became more vertical, requiring the climbers to use their hands and arms to help pull themselves up each step. They came to an area of solid smooth rock that was slightly less than vertical. In the center of the rock was a crack that lead up to the next outcropping. It was just wide enough for the climbers to gain a foothold and pull themselves up with their hands. Dedee thought that Thomas may have picked this route because he thought she would have a difficult time, but she matched Thomas step for step.

When they reached the outcropping, the ascent became less vertical, and Thomas said they would take a ten-minute rest. The men slouched down against a boulder, and Dedee talked to each one of them, encouraging them and reminding them that with each footstep, they were that much closer to freedom.

Thomas appeared to have forgotten his concern about Dedee's ability to keep up because he had stopped checking on her. He seemed to have grudgingly admitted to himself she was more than strong enough to meet the challenge of the Pyrenees.

Ian sat heavily, with his back against the big rock, still trying to catch his breath. His face was flushed pink, and sweat dripped off his chin, though the temperature had dropped dramatically as they climbed. He looked over at Dedee, who was rummaging through her backpack.

Thomas, who had walked over to a nearby ledge, signaled that someone was coming from the other direction, so they hid behind rocks and scrub. A sound, like rain pattering on a roof, got closer and closer. Thomas stood up, and Dedee's first thought was that he was going to betray them. Now she knew why she was suspicious of him. He must be a collaborator. She couldn't flee. Going down the rock face behind her would be more difficult than climbing it. The only other escape route was going forward, but that was blocked. Under her breath, she cursed and blamed herself for not vetting the guide more carefully. Then, from around a little bend in the path ahead, came a ewe, followed by a small herd of sheep. Thomas looked back at the others, saw their panicked faces relax, and laughed. They all laughed and moved on after the herd had passed.

Four days later, Dedee climbed the flight of stairs that led to the Consul's Office at the British Consulate in Bilbao. She wore a white blouse, a simple skirt, white socks, and plain black shoes. The consul's door was open, and as she entered, he put his pipe down and stood up to greet her. The office was large and smelled of fresh tobacco smoke. The consul was tall and lanky, and his tweed jacket had leather patches at the elbows that were worn through to the fabric. He squinted through steely gray eyes, and Dedee could not determine if his look was friendly or hostile.

"Mademoiselle de Jong?"

"Please call me Dedee," she said.

He motioned her to a chair and sat himself. "I have heard about you from our office in San Sebastián," he said. "Tell me about yourself."

"I've come from Brussels. I've brought you two Belgians who want to fight with the British and one Scottish soldier. We left Brussels last week and crossed the Pyrenees two nights ago."

The consul reached for his pipe and held it up, asking her with a raised eyebrow if she minded him smoking. He relit the pipe and puffed, looking over his reading glasses at Dedee. "Where are these three men you brought?" he asked.

"Downstairs."

He looked at her, incredulous. "How did you cross the mountains?"

"On foot, with a guide."

"You mean you just walked over the mountains? Forgive me, madam, but I find that very difficult to believe."

"I assure you that with the help of my guide Thomas, I hiked across those mountains. I may look too young or too small to you, but I'm as strong as a man and, being a girl, I attract less attention in the frontier zone. They never suspect women."

He stared at her thin arms, saying nothing.

Directly facing the consul, she said, "There are many downed airmen hiding in the Brussels area. Getting them back to fight another day is my mission. My father and I have established safe houses around Brussels where we can hide them until we can arrange to escort them to St. Jean de Luz. From there, we take them across the mountain passes, across the Bidassoa, and into Spain."

"Can you tell me more about how you accomplish all of that?" he asked.

"When a British plane gets shot down, usually the local people can get to them before the Germans do. With the help of the existing Belgian Resistance, we have tendrils throughout Belgium who can, with the help of local property owners, quickly locate and hide downed air crew. As quickly as possible, we move these airmen to various safe houses. The safe houses are owned by brave citizens who hide and feed the airmen until we move them again. We have trustworthy guides that take them from safe house to safe house until we get them to Brussels, where we give them identity papers and prepare them to travel by rail."

"Prepare them?" he asked.

"Yes. We instruct them on how to go through checkpoints and what to say if confronted by police. From Brussels, we transport them to Paris, where we give them French identifications and travel documents. When the timing is right, we move them by rail to the foot of the Pyrenees, where they are guided over the mountains to Bilbao."

The consul stood, and still puffing on his pipe, turned to look out his window. "What do you want from me?" he asked.

"We need money for guides, food, papers, and transportation."

"How much?"

Dedee was ready for this question and she rattled off the exact amounts. "It costs us six thousand Belgian francs per person from Brussels to St. Jean de Luc, and fourteen hundred pesetas for the guide, per trip".

When he reacted to the last number, she explained that the guides were nervous about taking Allied soldiers across, and they needed motivation.

The consul still looked doubtful. "How do I know you're not a German spy trying to infiltrate the Resistance?" he asked. "Can you prove you are what you claim to be?"

Dedee smiled. "Do I look like a German spy?"

He seemed to accept her answer. "I'll have to speak to my colleagues in our Madrid office," he said. "Can you return in two weeks?"

The consul gave Dedee the money for the Scotsman, and she went downstairs. She shook hands with the two Belgians and with Ian, who held her hand just a little longer.

"Good luck and God bless you," he said.

She wished him good luck as well and strode purposefully off, disappearing into the mass of office workers hurrying home in the late afternoon.

Dedee was disappointed that the consul had not accepted her more openly, and the disappointment brought tears to her eyes. She hoped he would have the necessary approval when she returned. She was proud of how she had crossed the mountains. The look on Thomas' face when he kept looking back and finding her still on his heels. She still worried about his loyalty. There was so much to do. She would need to lean heavily on Elvire to handle the details.

She took a train to San Sebastián, arriving just after noon, where Thomas was waiting to guide her back over the mountains. He suggested she rest the night and start early the next morning, but Dedee refused, and insisted she needed to get back as soon as possible. Thomas set a fast pace and the two of them, unencumbered by evaders, made good time. Dedee's legs were sore from the first crossing, but she never let on, and after a few miles, she got into the rhythm.

When she again arrived at Elvire's house, they discussed the capture of the ten Belgians and Miss Richards. The local carabineros could not be trusted, which reinforced her belief that her evaders had to be delivered directly to the British. Risking the lives of all the members of her line, only to have the 'packages' arrested at the border would not do. She would have to find a way to guarantee their safety once they entered Spain.

"Do you have any more bad news?" Dedee asked.

"Yes, I'm afraid I do," Elvire said. "My daughter Janine believes Arnold is in trouble. He is almost certainly arrested."

"Oh, my God," Dedee said in a whisper. "How?"

"She doesn't know. But she reasonably suspects a leak somewhere down the line."

Dedee was silent for a moment, then said, "An informer?"

They went to the backyard just before the sun set over the dark Pyrenees, and discussed the problems they faced. Elvire's husband, Fernand, joined them. Because he spoke fluent German, he was an interpreter for the local police in Anglet. When the conversation got around to their much-needed source for forged papers, he spoke up and told them he could help. Those forms were readily available at his local office. All he had to do was sneak them out.

∽

At the Madrid office of the British Embassy, Michael Cresswell read the communiqué from the consul in Bilbao. The idea of escorting the flyers over the western Pyrenees intrigued him. Another escape organization referred to as the Pat O'Leary Line that operated through Marseilles, had recently been compromised by the Gestapo, and no one was sure how effective they would be in the future. Everyone knew the German efforts to stop the flight of soldiers back to England were intensifying. Cresswell realized the final blessing for the payments the woman was asking for had to come from MI9 (Military Intelligence, Section 9) in Whitehall, who were charged by Churchill to facilitate the return of as many British soldiers as possible. Created in 1939, MI9 had become active in efforts to help escapers (those who had been caught) as well as evaders (those who were still evading capture).

Cresswell understood the politics of the home office better than anyone. Anticipating that some would think she was a German plant, he asked for a complete search of the files for anything they might have on Andrée de Jongh. Days later, he received a wire that reported the only thing they had about an 'Andrée de Jongh' was that she had written letters from Brussels to the families of soldiers wounded at Dunkirk the prior year. When the home office received this report, Dedee's story was accepted.

Cresswell then decided he wanted to help the woman as much as possible. With the final decision from MI9, he drove to Bilbao to talk with her on October 17, 1941.

When Dedee first met him at the local consul's offices, she was impressed with his demeanor. In addition, by driving all the way to San Sebastián, he had shown a personal interest in what she was doing. Unlike other Foreign Service types she had met, Cresswell was immediately supportive and knowledgeable about the challenges and dangers of escape and evasion work. He made it clear that the British government would reimburse her for each British soldier she presented, and also for the cost of the guides. Dedee wanted to be sure no strings were attached to the payments and that the money was just a reimbursement of her expenses. She also insisted that she remain in total control, with no British interference. She reasoned that British control meant red tape and delays in implementing her plans. She did not want to have to wait while some bureaucrat approved or disapproved her decisions.

Cresswell moved from behind his desk and they sat in comfortable chairs facing each other to talk.

"Your name is Andrée. So, why do they call you Dedee?" Cresswell asked.

"Dedee is a Belgian nickname for Andrée," she said.

"Oh, a code name, then," he said.

"Yes, it means literally 'little mother,'" she said smiling.

"Seems like everybody has to have a code name," he said. "Mine is Monday."

"Is that how I'm to refer to you?"

"Just in any correspondence you might have. And your code name will be 'Postman."

"Postman? Couldn't it be 'Postwoman?' I am a woman, after all."

He took a cigarette from a case and offered her one. She refused, and he lit up and leaned back in his chair. "Yes, I agree." he said with a wry smile.

Chapter 4

MAIDENHEAD, ENGLAND 1938

Sergeant Jack Newton lined up the bright yellow de Havilland Tiger Moth trainer for a landing directly into what little wind there was at the de Havilland School of Flying. The wind was variable, and with a front coming in, it shifted direction frequently. Jack eased back the power with his left-hand throttle. The little plane was very sensitive to air current changes, and Jack could feel the bumps as he neared the grass field. Clouds had been moving in from the west, but visibility was unlimited, and he felt comfortable. Approaching the fence, he brought the throttle back to idle. He could hear the wind blowing through the guy wires on the struts.

He was returning from an afternoon training session, and he enjoyed the plane's responsiveness as he pushed the left foot-operated aileron pedal to hold his plane's alignment with the runway as the wind changed direction. Sixty, fifty, forty, his speed bled off as he crossed the fence. The plane started to float in ground effect and Jack suddenly realized he was in an air pocket and he was going too fast. As he passed the midway portion of the field, he knew the safest thing to do was to hit the throttle and go around to try again, but he also thought his skill level was high enough to handle the situation, so he pushed the stick forward to force the two main wheels to the surface. A gust hit the plane from the right. Too late to correct, the downwind wheel hit hard, and the plane bounced. The wind caught the left wing, tilting it up severely. The opposite wing hit the runway, spinning the craft into a hard ground loop. The plane came to an abrupt halt, resting on its right wheel and wing, facing the wrong way.

Jack shut off the engine and took a deep breath. He climbed out of the cockpit and surveyed the damage. It had all happened so fast. Sixty seconds before, everything was perfect, and now it wasn't. His knees shook as he thought of the consequence of his failed landing and what it might mean to his lifelong desire to be a fighter pilot. But, then again, maybe the flight officer in the tower would realize the difficulty of this cross-wind landing and give him another chance. After all, no real harm had been done. Just some minor wing damage.

Jack had been born in north London in 1920, where his father was a chauffeur for a well-to-do industrialist. He always loved the expensive cars his father drove. They lived in a modest but comfortable flat above the garages until Jack was eleven. Then his father's boss moved them into a new house near the primary school, where Jack excelled in his studies.

Several years later, Jack became enamored of a new neighbor, Mary, who had moved in several houses away. They spent as much time together as Mary's parents would allow.

Jack passed his primary exams, and as his parents thought he had a mechanical aptitude, they sent him to the Regent Street Polytechnic School to study drawing and engineering. Upon graduation, he found a job with the Post Office, repairing switchboards and earning four shillings and sixpence a week.

In 1938, the specter of war was all anyone talked about. Neville Chamberlain had just returned from Germany after signing the Munich Agreement, which allowed Germany to annex the Sudetenland. Most of the English people viewed the agreement for what it was: a surrender to Adolph Hitler. Many saw war against Germany as inevitable. Caught up in the war fervor, Jack signed up with three of his buddies for the RAF Reserve.

The first parts of Jack's training were navigation and aerodynamics, and Jack did well. When he finally got into an airplane, his instincts were good, and the art of flying came easily. He was, however, partially colorblind.

At one point, he was given a light test, wherein he had to identify three differently colored lanterns. One was red, which he had no problem with. The other two, however, were pale green and amber. They looked exactly the same to him. When his superior asked him to point to the green light, Jack knew if he guessed wrong, he would never be a pilot. He took a deep breath and pointed to the one on the left, because he wore his wedding ring on that hand. He had guessed correctly.

The walk from his damaged plane to the tower was only several hundred yards, but to Jack it seemed to take forever. Several other pilots and a number of ground crew all stared at him as if they knew what was in store. The officer in the tower was a short, rotund man, who said tersely, "Your logbook, Sergeant."

Taking the logbook, he leafed through to the last page, picked up a pen, wrote a few lines, signed it, and handed it back to Jack with the page open. The man did not even look at Jack. Jack's heart sank when he saw that the man had written.

Sergeant Newton will most likely make a very proficient pilot, but not up to the standards required by His Majesty's Air Force.

Those few words meant he would never be a pilot in the RAF. The realization hit Jack like a sledgehammer. He turned to go. The officer had turned around. Jack hesitated, then realized any plea from him would go unheard, and walked out. He sat down on a bench outside and stared out at the airfield. Another pilot was landing a Tiger Moth, and Jack wished it was him. During his training he had fallen in love with flying. He loved the freedom. The idea that a man could take off and fly wherever he wanted had infected his being.

He decided that even if he couldn't be a pilot, he would become a gunner.

❧

Captain Roy Langlois announced "power on" and pushed the power levers full forward as the roaring, giant twin Rolls Royce Merlins bit the air, and twenty-eight thousand pounds of Wellington bomber, bombs, fuel, and crew slowly lumbered down the active runway at RAF Binbrook. Jack was ensconced in the front gunner's bubble turret with the three-bladed propellers just five feet from his ears. His turret, located twelve feet directly in front of the captain's windscreen, gave Jack a bird's eye view of the runway as the big plane picked up speed. The rear wheel came up and the plane's fuselage became horizontal, affording Jack an even better view. The bomber approached rotation speed, as the captain pulled back on the wheel, and the four-foot tires started to bounce. The thrill of flight always amazed Jack, as anything weighing nearly fourteen tons seemed impossible to lift into the air.

With the final bounce the "Wimpy," as it was called, jumped skyward, and the ride became instantly smooth.

Jack watched the ground disappear as they gained altitude. It was his first official bombing mission. He tugged one last time on his seatbelt apparatus when he felt a mild shudder as the big plane penetrated a layer of low lying scud clouds. His thoughts turned to the mission. His first official bombing raid. They were to join the other nine Wellingtons already in the air that made up the Twelfth Squadron. Their assignment was to hit the large tire manufacturing plants in Aachen, located two hundred-fifty miles southeast, near the German border with Belgium. The flight would be over the Strait of Dover and across Belgium to Aachen, where they would drop their ordnance and return home. The whole mission promised to be over in four or five hours.

Jack knew the front and rear gunner's positions on the Wellington were the most dangerous seats in the plane. The rear gunner was vulnerable when attacked by the German Messerschmidt 109 fighters, who usually approached from the rear. The rear gunner had four Browning 303s just for that reason. A single Browning could fire nearly twenty rounds a second. Multiply that by four, and an aware rear gunner could throw out an amazing amount of lead in a short period of time. The greatest peril for the front gunner was flak. The German anti-aircraft guns would set their ordnance to explode at the altitude they thought the enemy would be flying. The white-hot metal from the explosions could penetrate the gunner's plastic bubble with ease. Normally, Jack would be in the rear-gunner's turret, but the regular front gunner had asked if Jack wanted to change positions. The captain had agreed because gunnery school had taught them both positions. Jack was happy for a change of scenery.

The captain leveled off at twelve thousand feet, along with the rest of the squadron. Jack relaxed as the two big Merlin V-12's droned on. They were above the scattered layer of clouds and the moonlight reflected off the silvery cloud tops, giving the impression it was early morning and not midnight. Jack thought about Mary. Three months before, they had decided not to wait any longer to get married. Mary's parents had wanted them to wait until after the war was over because of the risks Jack would encounter as a bomber crewmember. British bombers faced the dual threat of being shot down by the Luftwaffe or the anti-aircraft batteries, which were especially effective as bombers neared big cities. Jack and Mary had decided to leave the problem to God, and were married and spent three nights honeymooning in the Cotswolds. Jack smiled as he remembered Mary's sweet voice. She loved Jack unabashedly, totally, and with no reservations.

The plane droned on.

"I can't see home anymore from back here," the rear gunner said.

"I see the coastline from up here," Jack said. They all knew what that meant.

"Gunners, clear your guns," came the announcement from the captain. "We're over the Dutch coast and we need to be one hundred percent."

Jack fired short blasts from both guns. "Guns cleared," Jack reported. The rear gunner did the same. The harsh, rapid recoil of the Brownings had brought Jack suddenly back to the cold, hard reality of their mission. He had learned to handle the big guns with a light grip because to do otherwise would send the vibrations through his whole body. The captain had told them to keep a sharp eye out for Jerries, and the realization that somewhere out there was a fighter pilot who wanted to kill him was sobering. The crew exchanged some light banter but their voices had an edge, and Jack knew they all had the same thoughts. Tension hung in the air like the darkness before a thunderstorm.

They flew on, Jack's senses on hyper alert. He could see searchlights ahead scanning for the squadron planes the German air defenses could surely hear. If a searchlight beam located and locked onto one of the Wellingtons, the flak guns would all concentrate on that one target and the hapless bomber would know what it felt like to be in front of a firing squad.

A shell-burst lit the night directly in front of Jack. The plane flew through the black smoke with a shudder that threw him up so hard he hit his head on the top of his turret even though his seatbelt was tight. Jack checked his plastic shroud. No apparent damage.

"That was a close one," Langlois shouted. "You okay, Jack?"

"Remind me to change my shorts when we get back," said Jack. He was amazed by the apparent speed of the bomber. With no clouds in the sky, a sense of the forward velocity of the plane was difficult to estimate, however, when they flew through the black flak, their speed of two hundred-thirty miles per hour revealed itself in a fast *whish*.

The flak explosions continued all around them. The captain ordered, "Open the bomb doors."

With a grinding clunk, the doors opened, and the plane again shuddered as they interrupted its slipstream.

"First target just ahead," the captain said to the bombardier. "Your airplane."

The bombardier was then able to control the aircraft and make minor adjustments in direction to ensure maximum accuracy. "Steady, left a bit, hold, hold...Bombs away!"

The thousand-pound bomb left the fuselage, and Jack felt his stomach drop as the plane leapt upward before the pilot could correct. Then the pilot maneuvered toward their second target, the Aachen railway yards. As the plane banked, Jack could see parts of the city burning. He had no idea if the fires were caused by the bomb his plane had dropped, but he had a brief sense of satisfaction just knowing all the damage below was caused by his squadron. Jack's attention was swiftly brought back to the present as more flak exploded nearby. Each explosion, if within one hundred yards or so, buffeted the plane as if they were flying through a cloud roiling with convection. As the plane leveled off, Jack thought at least they were headed toward England, and home, and Mary.

Again, the pilot said they were approaching the target and gave control to the bombardier, who tweaked their path then dropped the rest of their ordnance. "Bombs away," he announced and they all knew that they were homeward bound.

With the bomb doors closed, they flew out of the flak area, and Jack started to think that maybe this mission wasn't so bad after all. To Jack, the engines hummed a reassuring tune, seemingly happy to be powering the big plane with three-thousand pounds less weight. He took a deep breath of relief and continued to scan for Messerschmitts.

But Jack's relief was short lived.

With a thunderous *whap*, the big plane suddenly yawed hard to starboard.

One of the crew yelled, "What the hell was that?"

Jack saw flames from the starboard engine and the rhythmic throb of the two engines in sync changed to a roar as the enflamed engine raced in high RPMs. Jack knew it could blow at any second. The flames, fanned by the prop and forward speed of the aircraft, formed a ghostly comet tail extending aft from the crippled engine. Jack winced and leaned hard against the opposite side of his turret. He could feel the heat from the flames.

The captain immediately hit the starboard fire extinguisher button and the flames went out. But only briefly, as they immediately reignited. Langlois feathered the prop and shut down the engine to give the extinguishers a better chance. The three-bladed prop came to an abrupt halt with one blade pointing down. An omen of what was to come.

The "Wimpy" yawed hard to the right as the left engine was the only source of power. Jack stared in disbelief. The realization that the plane could not fly on one engine, even with its lightened load, slowly sank in.

How could things be so good one moment and so terrible the next? He looked down into the darkness and wondered how he could possibly survive. He thought of Mary.

As the plane lost altitude, so did his hopes.

The plane was in a slow descent. The captain had to use all of his strength to keep it flying in a straight line. With the right engine only serving as additional drag, he had to push the left rudder pedal hard, with his foot almost to the floor. The sharp-eyed wireless operator somehow tied a rope around the pedal and tied it off to reduce the captain's effort. The plane continued to sink.

The captain announced that he was heading for the Belgian coast and hoped that they could ditch in the North Sea. He didn't sound convinced. The whole crew knew the small dingy they carried was stowed just behind the charred engine and was most certainly burnt to a crisp.

Jack could now just make out the objects below. He could see a spire ahead and realized it was a church. *Must be Antwerp*, he thought. Then he realized the top of the spire was above the airplane.

"No choice. We'll land in the dark area just ahead," the captain said.

"God. We need a miracle," Jack said, as the plane neared treetop level.

Then, Jack didn't know it at the time, but the miracle was granted.

"Captain! Just over to our port. You see it?" Jack exclaimed. "Is that an airfield?"

"Roger that, Jack. Let's try it," the captain said.

The crew felt the plane shudder as it attempted the difficult task of turning toward the only good engine. The plane wallowed, struggling to maintain enough airspeed to avoid a full stall. The captain jammed his left aileron to the floor, coaxing the wounded bird slowly around. He could not turn his landing lights on for fear of being discovered by the Germans and being shot down before he could land. He calculated the field was darkened because of the air-raid alerts. As he lined up for the runway, he pulled out and flipped down the landing gear lever.

Jack felt the clunk of the gear down and locked, and almost immediately the tires squealed as the plane touched down. The landing was one of the smoothest Jack had ever experienced. He silently thanked the captain and his RAF trainers who had obviously done their job. He felt the mild vibration of the big tires on the runway through his seat, and briefly thought he had never expected to ever land on a German runway.

"Everybody out," said the captain, braking the plane to a stop and shutting down the engine.

They deplaned and gathered around the captain.

They thought they would have been welcomed by German airport guards, but, unbelievably, none were in sight. From a distance, they could hear the sound of racing engines.

"Let's burn the plane and get outta here," the captain said. Everyone understood it was standard procedure, even if it meant letting the whole town know they were there. Using a flare as a lighter, the crew threw their unneeded parachutes into the plane and set them ablaze. Then they set off across the field as fast as their heavy leather flying suits and boots would allow. They crossed the barbed-wire periphery of the airport and ran for another fifteen minutes.

Thoroughly winded, the captain motioned for them to stop in a copse of trees. They looked back and saw the glow of their burning Wimpy. With still no sign of German activity, the captain decided they should split into two groups to improve their chances of not getting caught.

"Jack, you and Tich are with me, and the rest of you head out in that direction," Langlois said, pointing to the south.

"Good luck, Skip," the co-pilot said, and the two small groups departed.

Jack felt relieved that he was with the captain. He had won the Distinguished Flying Cross before the war. He never mentioned it, but everyone knew.

Jack's three crewmates disappeared into the darkness. He would not see any of them until after the end of the war.

Richard Copley, nicknamed 'Tich," was the radio operator. Jack did not know him well, but he knew he was well qualified to be a part of their crew. Tich got his nickname because he was barely five feet tall, which allowed him to move around the inside of the Wimpy without ducking his head.

The captain seemed to be heading southwest, but Jack was not sure if he knew where he was going. During their training, they had been taught a few basics about what to do if they had to ditch in occupied country. They were told to look for a church, and possibly the minister would have advice for them. They each were supplied with Belgian, Dutch, and French money; about two pounds' equivalent of each. They also had small compasses hidden in their smoking pipes.

The captain kept on at a fast pace. Jack could feel his legs losing energy, and he wondered how much longer he would be able to keep up. He was tall and wiry, and he thought he was in relatively good shape, but the captain and Tich showed little indication of the fatigue he was feeling. With no sign of Germans, Jack's adrenalin levels diminished. He started to think about where he was and the deep trouble he was in. Briefly, he thought about Mary. How would she know he was alive? What if he was caught and imprisoned? Would she know? Would she wait? The tension of the unknown was overwhelming.

They stopped on the edge of a corn field. The corn had been cut and stacked into neat rows of shocks. Looking back, they could see morning light to the east.

"We better hide," the captain said, and he crawled into the bottom of one of the shocks. He instructed Jack and Tich to do the same and to stay there until nightfall. Jack picked a shock next to the captain. He knew they would be under there for quite a while, so he made a circular nest for himself. He lay down, utterly exhausted. His flight suit was wet with sweat on the inside, but the leather kept him warm nonetheless. Lying on his side, he could feel the lumpy soil against his hips and ribcage. Slowly, his breathing became regular. Even though he was exhausted, he couldn't fall asleep. He wondered if Mary was thinking about him. He heard the captain snoring in his shock, but he could tell Tich was having a hard time getting comfortable. Jack could hear him shifting corn stalks around. Then he heard Tich crawl out and, between the stalks, saw him prop himself against a tree by the road. Then Jack finally fell asleep.

Jack awoke as the early morning light penetrated his shock. He was cold. He looked out and saw Tich standing to relieve himself. Then he heard the screech of a bicycle brake and saw a boy staring at Tich.

"Bonjour. Allo," the boy said. "Are you an English airman?"

Tich looked speechless, but the captain, who had been awakened by the noise, came out of his shock. "Yes, we are, and we could use your help."

Jack was surprised that the captain would put his trust in the boy so quickly.

The boy stood up straight, "I am with the Resistance, and I will get help," he said proudly. He went back to his bicycle and told them to wait until dark. He rode off down the road, disappearing over a slight hill.

"What'll we do now, Captain?" Jack asked.

"He could come back tonight with help or he could be back in an hour with a German patrol," said Tich.

"He couldn't have been more than fifteen years old," said the captain. He hesitated. "If we run now, we risk being seen by somebody more likely to do us harm than that young man. We really have no choice. I vote we stay, what do you men think?"

Both Jack and Tich agreed.

"We have twelve to thirteen hours until dark. We're going to have to crawl back under our shocks and stay hidden until then. And, Copley, you need to stay under there this time and not show your face," the captain ordered.

"I've learned my lesson," Tich said, crawling into a different shock.

Jack could not go back to sleep. He tried all the little tricks he used to use, but none worked. One of his favorite ways to try to sleep was to go over his Tiger Moth mishap in his mind. He remembered every single maneuver he'd tried that day, and usually, by the second or third time, he would be asleep. But this time, he just got mad at himself. He heard an occasional bicycle passing by on the road, and once he heard a heavy truck, which he guessed might be a load of German soldiers looking for them. He did not know that when the Germans finally found their burned Wellington, they initially assumed that the crew had perished in the fire. Only later were they able to search the charred wreckage and determine no bodies were in the plane. Jack thought that the longer the Jerries didn't show up looking for them, the more likely the boy could be trusted.

Only when the sun was finally well below the western horizon did he hear the captain rattle his shock and tell him the boy was back.

The boy said, "You come with me," and he nervously led them onto the narrow road, which proved to be not much more than a country lane. Jack still thought the boy was in his mid-teens. He wore glasses, and his dark hair almost hung over his eyes in front. They learned his name was Richard Dumoulin.

Shortly, Richard turned into a farmyard and introduced the three of them to Alphonse de Voegt and his wife. In broken English, the farmer asked if they were the airmen who had landed at Duerne Airfield the night before. He informed them that the Germans were searching the entire countryside for them. The farmer assured them they would be safe up in the hayloft of his barn. Mrs. de Voegt packed two baskets of food including sandwiches, cheese, and fruit while Mr. de Voegt gathered blankets and pillows.

After showing the three airmen to the hayloft, Mr. de Voegt closed the trapdoor through which they had entered and told them to rest, and that they would be moved out the next morning.

The loft was a large area above the barn's livestock pen that contained loose hay from which de Voegt fed his livestock every morning. When the door closed, the loft was darkened, but enough light seeped through the barn's siding for them to see.

"Did you guys think Monsieur de Voegt was suspicious of us?" Tich asked.

"Suspicious of what?" Jack asked lying down in the hay.

"Maybe they think we're German spies," Tich said. "If we were, the de Voegts would be in deep trouble."

"You're right, Tich," the captain said. "Put yourself in his shoes. If a soldier came to your door asking for help and you said 'yes,' you would be endangering the lives of your whole family. You could say 'no' and there would be no risk. The de Voegts have chosen to say 'yes' put their lives on the line. They have every damned right to be suspicious."

The three airmen spent the rest of the day in the loft, telling stories and recounting their experiences in flight school. Their flight suits kept them warm, and they slept soundly that night.

Jack opened his eyes as the early morning light plied through cracks in the barn siding. The sounds of a farm: the bleat of a sheep, the crow of a rooster, milk being stripped into a pail. He looked over at the captain, whose eyes were also open. They looked at each other with the mutual unspoken realization that nothing had changed since the night before and they really were in occupied enemy territory. They were still in deep trouble and they both knew it.

M. de Voeght took them to the farmhouse, where they were well fed, and after breakfast, they were taken into another room where clothes were piled on the floor. In broken English, he instructed them to get rid of all their clothing and pick out some things that fit, which they did.

Jack, being well over six feet tall, had a hard time finding pants that were long enough, but he finally donned a pair of well-worn woolen tweeds and a brown beret.

That evening, a young girl came to the house, and M. de Voeght told them they were being transferred to Antwerp. After thanking them for their help, they followed the girl, each keeping a distance behind the other. They had been instructed to keep their heads down and not to speak to anyone, even if spoken to.

Over an hour later, they reached the outskirts of the city. As they approached a tram station, Jack saw a group of German soldiers with their rifles slung over their backs. He hesitated. He couldn't take his eyes off the soldiers, who were laughing and talking among themselves. He pulled his beret down over his eyes. The enemy was just ten feet away. Looking the other way, he leaned up against a light post and took several deep breaths to quell his fear.

A tram came, and the soldiers got on, never even looking his way. Even though the air was cool, Jack could feel his armpits were wet. A while later, another tram came, and the girl signaled this was the one. They had been given tram tickets before they left the farm, and Jack sat down several seats behind the girl. As the tram proceeded, Jack had time to realize his tweed pants were irritating his skin. At first, he thought the wool fabric must have been infested with fleas, but when he pulled up his pant leg, he could see that the irritation was caused by the coarse material. The situation was made much worse because when he had picked out his new clothes, he had been unable to find any underwear that fit.

The tram made four stops before the girl stood and they followed her off. No one gave any of them a second look. After walking for twenty minutes or so, the girl led them to a large house owned by a banker by the name of Duquenne. The three of them were ensconced in a large room on the second floor, which made them quite comfortable. They were told they would be moving on the next day.

That night at dinner, they learned from M. Duquenne that the Germans were on a frantic search to find them. Roadblocks had been set up on main arteries, and were frequently moved. Airplanes had been deployed. Patrol boats searched the coastlines.

As the search for the downed crew intensified, fear rose among the Resistance that Jack, the captain, and Tich could be spies. Even the de Voeghts had seemed suspicious. The captain was right, they came to realize the truth that anyone who helped them would be shot if they were, in fact, spies. The Germans had planted fake airmen before, in attempts to identify the families that were aiding the evaders, but fortunately, the fakes had been obvious and hadn't fooled anybody.

The airmen were moved the next day to another safe house in the nearby town of Liege. There they met Emile Witmeur, who was the head of the Resistance organization in that area, nicknamed the Liege Beaver-Baton Resistance organization. Witmeur was himself an ex-pilot from the Belgian Air Force. In fluent English, he told the three airman of the need to absolutely verify whether or not they were the downed aircrew. He left little doubt that if they were determined to be spies, they would be shot. The questioning would start the next day. In the meantime, they were locked in separate rooms and forbidden to talk to one another.

Jack heard the key turn, bolting his door from the outside, and turned and looked around the small bedroom, which was evidently that of a young boy. A poster showing a British Spitfire with its captain standing next to it was tacked to the wall. If it hadn't been for the air pocket with the Tiger Moth, it could have been him in the picture. There were several miniature toy cars on a table next to the bed. Jack had some just like them when he was a boy. Jack sat down on the bed and let the enormity of his situation overwhelm him. What if he answered some questions wrong? He had always thought if he were to get shot, it would be by the enemy, not the Resistance. Then, he wondered how they would know whether the answers to their questions were right or wrong. How would they know?

Early the next morning, Witmeur entered Jack's room. He was young, Jack guessed around twenty years old, with penetrating blue eyes. He carried a file folder on a tray that also held some scones and two cups of coffee. His demeanor was all business. He sat in a chair across from Jack.

"Good morning, Newton," he said. "Care for some coffee?"

Jack was on guard immediately. 'Newton?' It was 'Jack' yesterday, he thought. He reached for some coffee, but his hands shook so badly he decided not to have any. He waved his hands in refusal.

"Nothing to be nervous about," Witmeur said. "This shouldn't take too long. We just want to get the truth. Shall we get started?"

Witmeur opened his file folder without waiting for an answer. "You've told us you were a gunner on your Wellington the night you were shot down. Is this correct?"

When Jack answered affirmatively, Witmeur wrote in the file.

"Were you the nose gunner or tail gunner?"

"Nose gunner, but—"

"Just answer the question, please," Witmeur cut in. "Number and caliber of your guns?"

"Four Browning .303s."

Witmeur looked up.

"I mean two .303s."

"Which is it, Newton? Four or two?"

"Two, sir, I just…"

"Just answer the question, Newton," he cut in again. "Who made the turret?"

"Vickers."

Witmeur looked up again and stared at Jack.

"I—I mean Frazer-Nash."

"You sure?"

Jack took a deep breath. "Yes."

The questions came in a steady stream for the next several hours. Most were about the Wellington and crew, and Jack, once he settled in, answered them all. He regretted his early stumbling, which had been caused by the fact that he was normally a tail gunner.

Witmeur left, and Jack assumed it was to ask the others similar questions, but in the afternoon, he came back, and the questioning continued, on a totally different tack.

"Your address in England, Newton?"

Jack replied.

He was asked many basic questions about his service and family.

Then Witmeur asked, "What is the name of the road at the end of the road you live on?"

Jack answered quickly. He could also see that Witmeur was losing what little patience he had previously displayed.

"What color was your house?"

"Red brick."

"And your bedroom?"

Jack opened his mouth to answer, but stopped himself. He thought it was yellow, but it might have been light green.

Witmeur looked up, staring. "What color is your bedroom?"

"Yellow."

Witmeur wrote in his notebook for a few minutes, then he looked up and told Jack his questioning was over. He rose and left the room. Sometime later, the captain and Tich came in. Their questioning was over, also. At least they were together, although the door was locked again.

They talked about the questions, and Jack determined he was the only one who thought he hadn't known all the answers. He told them that he wasn't all that familiar with the front turret on the Wellington because it was the first time he'd ever been there. Then he relayed that he didn't even know the color of his bedroom, and explained his colorblindness and how he had guessed to get accepted as a pilot. The captain explained what he thought was going to happen, thinking that the Resistance must have a radio, and they would give the questions and answers back to the Brits for confirmation. He figured they should hear in the morning.

That night, the captain and Tich went quickly to sleep. Their snoring sounding like two Bristol radial engines out of sync. Jack lay awake wondering if he would face a firing squad in the morning.

The next morning, Witmeur unlocked their door and entered. He looked first at the captain. "Your story has been verified." He shook the captain's hand.

Then he addressed Tich. "Your story has been verified. Thank you." He shook his hand.

He stepped in front of Jack, standing erect. "We've had some problems with your story, however, Newton."

Jack's heart sank into his stomach.

"Your mother says you're colorblind, Jack. Why didn't you tell us?" A broad smile broke out on his face and he offered Jack his hand.

"Because you didn't give me a chance," Jack said, smiling.

"Now let's get you guys back to England so you can give them some more of what you gave them in Aachen," Witmeur said.

"What do you mean?" the captain asked.

"You guys blew the tire factory to smithereens," Witmuer said. "You shut them down for good. They won't be making tires in that place again. Really nice job."

For the three crewmen, the news of their success was like icing on the cake.

"What will we do? Take a night boat ride across the channel?" Tich asked.

"That's the last thing. The Jerries have patrols all over. Even if we could find somebody to take you over, you'd be shot out of the water before we got out of sight of the Belgian coast," Witmuer said.

"How we will get back?" Tich asked.

"Through France and across the Pyrenees to Gibraltar," Witmuer said. "We've got an entire line set up to take care of you. It's called the Comet Line. We're just the top part of it. We gather the downed fliers and deliver them to our boss, and then we're done."

"Your boss?" said the captain.

"Yep. We'll have you transferred in a few days. Meantime, we have a lot of work to do," Witmuer said.

That estimate of 'a few days' turned out to be optimistic. First, Jack had to say goodbye to the captain and Tich, as they were separated. Then, Jack, alone, was moved from safe house to safe house over the next several weeks. He perceived that, while the Resistance was comfortable with his authenticity, the pressure from the Gestapo was growing even more intense.

On a rare, frosty morning in early September, Jack was transferred to a house in Waterloo owned by Max and Celine Evrards. The notable thing about this house was that it had been requisitioned by the German Army to house two young Nazi bike patrol soldiers. The Evrards lived on the first floor of the house with their small Westland terrier, while the two soldiers lived upstairs. Jack was consigned to the basement. It was a single dark, damp, windowless room with a military style cot and a single lamp in the corner. Luckily, the Evards had some books, one of which was an English translation of *War and Peace*. It took Jack a week to read it.

The terrier hated anyone in uniform. It barked incessantly whenever the two Germans came into or left the house. This

proved beneficial to Jack. He knew to hide and stay quiet whenever the dog started yapping. The two soldiers had an MP-40
Schmiesser submachine gun that they carried on their bike, and
whenever they came off their patrols, they would carry the heavy
gun up the steps, leaving a trail of oil. As they hoisted the heavy
gun up the steps, the dog would nip at their ankles, and the soldiers would use the foulest language to express their displeasure.

Shortly, however, the duo was transferred, and Jack moved
upstairs into much more comfortable surroundings. Weeks went
by, and the fact that he was penned in weighed upon him. He
was told not to go near the windows when he was out of the basement, and he yearned for fresh air. In the back of the Evrards'
house was a small garden surrounded by a wooden fence. On
one bright, sunny afternoon, the call of the outdoors became
too much. Jack looked out the kitchen door onto the garden. He
reasoned that no one would see him if he just went out to take a
look and breathe some fresh air.

He opened the back door and walked out, scanning the area
to be sure no one else was about. Seeing no one, he stepped into
the garden and breathed in the aromas of the rich earth and
plants. His mind started to wander as he stopped to admire each
planting. As he got to the back of the garden, he saw a little gate
that went out into the countryside. Without thinking, he walked
through the gate and down a little path that followed a hedge-
row. As he rounded a corner, he almost bumped into a German
soldier who was facing the other way, smoking a cigarette. Jack
froze. Should he attack the man or run? He chose the latter and
quickly turned back.

"Halt!" The German came running with his rifle pointed in
his direction.

Jack stopped in his tracks. The soldier approached. "Aus-
weispapiere jetzt!" *Identity papers, now!* he demanded.

Jack stared at the soldier blankly, his mind reeling. If he ran,
he would be shot. If he told the German the truth, he would be

shot. Almost reflexively, he punched the soldier in the face. The man's helmet flew off and his legs crumpled under him.

Jack ran back to the Evrards' house. They came home just as he entered, and he told them what had happened and apologized profusely for his stupidity. They eyed the knuckles on Jack's right hand, which dripped blood onto his shoes. Jack held his hand up, realizing he must have hit the hapless soldier very hard indeed. The Evrards immediately contacted the Resistance, knowing he had to leave the area as soon as possible. Fortunately, the Germans thought the assailant had been a vagrant passing by, and they never questioned the Evrards.

Over the next few days, Jack was transferred to several more safe houses. During this time, he learned that the captain and Tich had been captured in Brussels. They had been found in a sewer, trying to escape the city. Jack was devastated.

At that time, Jack was joined by Larry Birk, a pilot from Australia. The two of them were told they were about to be transferred to the main part of the Comet Line, and the apparatus that would escort them back to England. Over the next few days, Jack and Larry were supplied with falsified papers, which they were told would stand up to all but the very tightest scrutiny by the Gestapo. His new passport said he was Jacques Dumonceau, a businessman from Southern France. When he flipped it over, he saw his picture, which they had taken only days before. In it he was wearing the same jacket he'd selected from the pile of clothing at the de Voeghts, so many weeks before. To Jack, it felt like a lifetime.

The next morning, they would finally depart Belgium, cross the Somme, and proceed by rail to the Pyrenees. Jack would meet the person who would have the most profound effect on him for the rest of his life.

Chapter 5

NOVEMBER 1941

Dedee could hear the voices of the three men before she entered the room. They were laughing and sharing stories of their experiences as evaders in Belgium. When Dedee came in, all three were sitting on the side of a bed, and the smiles on their faces disappeared. She knew that to them, she looked no more than a teenager.

"Hello. It's Jack, Larry, and Howard, isn't it?" she said.

The room was stone silent. Finally, Jack said, "Yes, that's right, ma'am."

"I'm Larry. Australian."

"I'm Howard Carroll," said the third, almost as if it was a question.

"My name is 'Andrée,' but you will call me 'Dedee,' which means 'Little Mother,' and I will be your 'Little Mother' until I deliver you to the British consulate in Spain."

"You mean *you're* taking us across the Pyrenees?" Howard asked.

"The Germans have made the channel crossing very dangerous. They have patrols everywhere, and if they find evaders or escapees within a mile of the coast, they shoot first and ask questions later. The southern route, while it can be precarious, is much safer."

The three stared at each other.

"So, we'll take a train to the foothills, you'll drop us off, and then we hike over?" asked Jack.

"That's right, Jack. But I'll be with you every step of the way. I'll see you early in the morning, when we leave for Corbie, to cross the Somme. Get some rest, gentlemen."

She turned and left, closing the door softly. She smiled, knowing exactly what was going through the men's minds. A petite young woman was probably not the kind of person they had envisioned. It was a repeating story, and Dedee was getting used to it. She knew they would change their minds well before they arrived in Spain.

The next morning at breakfast, Dedee could still see the doubt on their faces. She told them some of the dangers they might encounter and how they must follow her instructions faithfully. She said that she had not failed in any of her attempts, and she didn't plan to fail this time. Her tone was reassuring, and she could see the men relax a little.

"We've been cooped up for quite a while," said Jack, "and I worry about my ability to climb across the mountains. I haven't had any real exercise for three months."

"You'll do it," she said with confidence. "Don't worry."

She told them the rules and asked them to practice being silent again. If any of them inadvertently spoke, any German within hearing range would become suspicious.

"Why don't I just become a mute?" asked Jack.

"We've tried mutes before, and they work well. However, more mutes might raise too many eyebrows," she said. "You can appear to be reading a paper or sleeping. But you cannot speak. So, let's practice. I'll leave the room for a few minutes. Practice not speaking."

She left the room and closed the door. Then she put her ear to the door and listened. They did not say anything, but she suspected they were mouthing words. Ten minutes later, she went back into the room. She looked at her watch, then asked in English, "Who has the time?"

They all looked at their watches.

"You cannot fall into a trap like that," she said. "You do that on a train or in a café and we're all caught. It's a favorite tactic of theirs. By the way, none of your watches are made in Europe. Get rid of them. I want the three of you to become French, so please start thinking like Frenchmen. Like Frenchmen who do not talk."

Dedee described various situations and how they should respond. She told them they would be leaving soon and left the room.

The men were impressed. Jack, in particular, admired her for her organization and intelligence. He thought about crossing the Pyrenees with her and how he would feel if she could make it and he couldn't. He found himself looking forward to spending time with her.

Their train to the French/Belgian border departed in the late afternoon. As they left the safe house, Dedee made the simple announcement, "Gentlemen, let's go. I'm going to take you home."

The trip to the border town of Quievrain took ninety minutes and was uneventful, as were the next two tram rides to Corbie. Darkness had settled by the time they made their way to the Somme. The water was somewhat lower than when Dedee had last crossed, and the three men were able to walk across, through water up to their chests. The water was cold and took Jack's breath away. None of them realized that Dedee had to swim. She just glided along in the water, encouraging each of them forward.

When they reached on the other side, Nennette was waiting for them. She escorted them to her house a short distance away, where they would spend the night. Upon entering her house, they met a fourth 'package,' Gerard Waucquez, a Belgian explosives expert. The British wanted him back in England, where he would later be air dropped back into France to help with the demolition of bridges before the invasion everyone knew was coming.

Nennette's house was more like a river cabin, with three rooms: a kitchen/living area and two bedrooms. A cozy fire helped the four of them dry their clothes while they enjoyed hot coffee, rich with heavy cream. The four evaders slept in one bedroom while Dedee curled up in front of the fireplace.

In the morning, the train ride from Amiens to Paris was uneventful, but when they arrived, they learned their express train to Bayonne was delayed for three hours. Just outside the train station was a theater that showed German propaganda films, and Dedee decided that would be a good place to kill time. Dedee and Gerard sat together and the other three found seats a short distance away. The film started with the song, *Erika*, sung by a male choir. The drums pounded out the music, which accompanied images of cannons in combat, with each drumbeat coinciding with the cannons' discharge. Then came the reels of thousands of German soldiers marching into Paris, with the swastika flying over the Eiffel Tower. Then Hitler speaking in front of a grand march in Berlin, with his hands in the air. Dedee's four boys could not understand German, but each time 'Sieg Heil' was yelled by the soldiers in the film, Jack and the others would stand, raise their right arm in salute, and yell the same 'Sieg Heil,' clicking their heels. Dedee frowned, but she knew the boys were just blowing off steam. She felt the weight of their safety squarely on her shoulders. She was achieving her dream. Jack would be her first RAF flier to be delivered to the consulate. She hoped.

All five boarded the same train car. The coach, because it was an express, was compartmentalized, with a hallway down the right side of the car. Each compartment had seating for eight, and Dedee had previously told them they would all sit in the same compartment. She entered a compartment with Gerard, and as she opened the door, she caught Jack's eye and signaled that this was where she wanted them all to sit. Jack would sit next to the window on one side of the two facing bench seats, while Dedee sat near the door with Gerard next to her. They didn't speak or acknowledge each other. Larry sat opposite Dedee. Two older ladies came in and sat across from each other next to Jack.

A flagman ran past the window, a shrill whistle blew, and the train slowly started to move, gathering speed as the steam from the engine spewed skyward. The the wheels settled into rhythm as they moved through the Paris suburbs. The sights of an occupying army were clearly visible through the large windows. Tanks, cannon, and all kinds of ordnance were seemingly stockpiled everywhere. Swastika flags flew from all the larger buildings and stations.

As the train moved out into the countryside, the door opened and a French train official, leaned in, accompanied by a German soldier.

"Billet?" the Frenchman asked.

Each person presented his or her ticket and papers to the train official, who looked at them and handed them to the German. After a cursory inspection, the German returned them with a polite, "Danke."

Dedee relaxed. *Maybe this won't be that difficult,* she allowed herself to think.

Sometime later, a man opened the door with an unlit cigarette in his hand. He looked at Larry, asking for a light in German. Larry didn't respond. Then he asked in French and Larry still didn't respond.

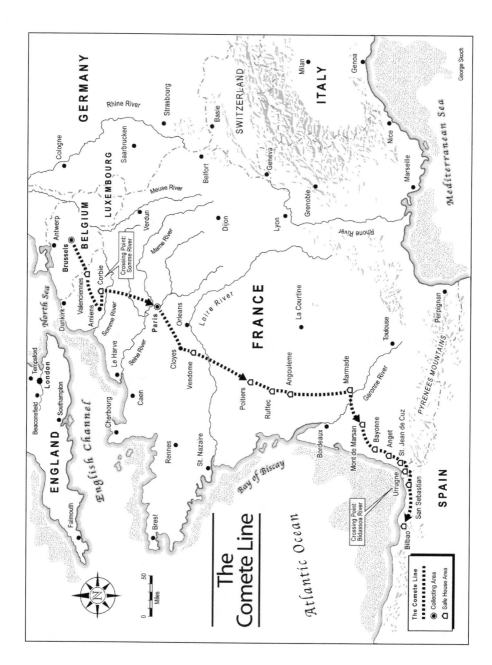

The Comete Line

"Oh, darling," Dedee said in French. "There you go daydreaming again. The gentleman wants a light. Give me your lighter." She flicked her fingers at Larry, indicating a lighter, which he immediately gave her. When she lit the man's cigarette, Jack smiled and closed his eyes as if to sleep. The man took a deep draw and closed the door. Dedee sat back. *One thing at a time,* she thought to herself as the train rambled toward the Pyrenees.

Dedee surveyed her 'packages.' She was living up to her code name. She smiled, remembering her conversation with Cresswell. She considered her charges. Larry was a bit of a loose cannon. He was a little like Ian, and her biggest worry. Gerard was no problem. He could speak and act the way she needed him to. Then there was Jack, whose face was hidden behind *Le Figaro.* They had had a long conversation at Nennette's cottage. She was confident he could handle most situations, and even though he feared he wasn't strong enough to get over the mountains, she knew he could. He had a self-effacing way about him that she found attractive. He was a gentleman's gentleman, and Dedee thought he probably dearly loved his new wife. He was almost boyish in his manner, like an overgrown kid, but he had a stiff backbone, an inner resilience that exuded confidence without braggadocio. He was tall and slender and sported a fine mustache. She sighed, then scolded herself for letting her mind wander. She could not get emotionally involved with a 'package,' she would be endangering her whole mission if she did.

The train slowed and she snapped out of her trance. They were approaching Bayonne. She stood to look out the window. As the train veered suddenly as if it was crossing a spur, she fell sideways, one hand hitting the window and the other finding Jack's knee. She quickly righted herself and withdrew her hand. Jack smiled at her.

Dedee stepped off the train into the cool morning air. She walked with Gerard. Jack, Larry, and Howard followed, spaced out so each could follow the other at a distance. Walking on the crowded platform toward the station, Dedee saw three German soldiers marching fast, almost running, straight toward them with their rifles held in front of them as if ready for action. She watched nonchalantly as they approached, but inwardly, she feared the worst. The three soldiers came right at the two of them, split, and went past. She couldn't help but look back to see if they were after any of her 'packages.' Being unable to see over the throngs of travelers, she looked to Gerard, who was taller. A moment later, he murmured not to worry, and they walked on.

When they approached the exit, Dedee saw a large group of Gestapo agents crowded around the checkpoint where travelers presented their papers, whether they were entering the platform or exiting. Dedee saw one of the passengers who had been on their car pulled off by the Germans and roughly hauled away. She stopped. Something was going on and she didn't want any of her charges' papers to be scrutinized too closely. There was always the chance an alert agent would recognize them as forgeries and sound the alarm. She took Gerard's arm and guided him into a small café located immediately adjacent to the checkpoint. The other three followed and sat at a nearby table.

Gerard ordered coffee for five. The ruckus at the checkpoint continued, and Dedee looked for another way out of the station. Just then, Elvire's only daughter, Janine, appeared, walked up to Dedee, and whispered in her ear. She had found another way in and out of the station through the lavatories. It was a back door that was normally locked, but Janine had used her charm to get a key from the custodian. They finished their coffees and exited the station with the guards none the wiser.

From the station, they boarded a tram for the short ride to Anglet, where they arrived at Elivre's cottage around mid-morning. The sun was bright when they entered the cottage.

Hidden from the road by tall trees and hedges, the dwelling offered spectacular views of the Pyrenees. Jack looked in awe at the towering peaks that served as a natural barrier between Spain and France. The peaks rose steeply, and the morning sun reflected off the rocks, creating an image that looked impregnable to human travel.

"Looks impossible," Jack said to Dedee, standing on Elvire's front porch. "Is that snow I see on top?"

"Not impossible," Dedee said. "We'll take it one step at a time and be over before you know it. Yes, there will be some snow, but not much."

The four men settled in. The weather forecast called for heavy rain at lower elevations starting in the afternoon and lasting for several days. They were instructed to stay inside the house; however, because of the dense foliage around the cottage, they could roam from room to room without worrying about being seen through the windows.

Janine had heard from Dedee's father that the Gestapo had visited him, looking for Dedee. Paul had told them he didn't know where she was, and when questioned more closely, he told them that she was a young woman and he could not keep track of her every movement, which seemed to temporarily placate the officers. Dedee was stunned to hear this news. She could not possibly imagine how the Gestapo had learned her father's address in Brussels.

Elvire, Janine, and Dedee sat on lounge chairs in back of the cottage. A light breeze rattled the leaves at the tops of the old oak trees. There was a sense of timelessness. Those same oak trees had been there for scores of years. They would probably even outlast the war. She had to do her part to make certain those trees would again shelter a free people.

Elvire was sitting on the edge of her chair as if waiting for an opportune time to speak. "Arnold is missing," she said. "We think he was captured."

"Oh, Elvire, I'm so sad to hear that. Are you sure?" Dedee asked.

"He was on a raid organized by the Resistance. They were trying to blow up a fuel depot. The Germans were tipped off. Several escaped, but Arnold wasn't one of them," Elvire said.

"We have to assume he was captured. No telling what they will do to him."

"So, you think Arnold will be forced to talk," Dedee said.

"Yes. You cannot go back to Brussels," Janine said. "They'll throw you in prison."

Dedee stared at Elvire for a moment, the significance sinking in. "If he is tortured," she said. "No way can we guess what he might say."

"I agree," Elvire said. "But he won't tell them everything. He's smart. He knows you will not be home, so he might give the Gestapo the Brussels address. He'll probably tell them your father is not involved. But that might come out later if they continue to torture him. The Gestapo will check and recheck. They're going to figure this out."

"We must tell Paul to get out of Brussels," Dedee said.

Paul had set up the Brussels headquarters for the escape line in his office at the school where he was an administrator. They reasoned that no one would suspect an organization of that sort to be operating out of a school for young children.

Dedee knew the Brussel's operation was very important, but she could not expose Paul to the risk of being caught. The British bombing of Germany was picking up steam, and a corresponding number of downed bombers and fighters meant that dozens and even hundreds of Allied fliers needed their help. She would handle the problem when she returned from San Sebastián.

"Here's to the rain stopping," Jack said, raising his water glass at dinner.

"I'll drink to that," said Gerard. "By the way, does it always rain here in Anglet?"

Elvire explained that when the upper wind currents swept across Spain and were then lifted up to cross the mountains, the air would cool and rain would fall. That the heavy rains they were getting now were not exceptional and would last several days.

Dedee knew that her four 'packages' were anxious to get to freedom. The way Jack had looked at the mountains, she thought, he must feel very close to getting home. The news of the delay sank in, and while no one complained, their disappointment hung in the air like a bad omen.

Hoping to lighten the mood, Dedee asked, "Larry, what's the first thing you're going to do when you get home?"

"Oh, I don't know," Larry said in a monotone. "Just want to get there, first."

"What about you, Jack?" she asked.

"I thought our weather in England was bad, but this—" he said.

When she saw that her efforts to cheer the boys up were failing, Dedee announced it was time for bed.

In the bedroom, the men stood awkwardly, waiting for Dedee to tell them what to do. They didn't have any bedclothes, so they just looked at her in embarrassment.

The cottage had only two bedrooms. The first was where Elvire and Fernand slept. The second was a large room with a single, very large bed with brass knobs on the headboard and huge pillows.

Jack said, "Dedee should sleep in the bed and the rest of us on the floor."

"The bed is quite large," Dedee said. "We can all sleep together. I will not have you sleeping on the floor. You need all the rest you can get for the journey ahead."

The four men looked at each other, wondering how that would work.

"It'll be simple," Dedee added. She turned to Larry and Howard. "You two are unmarried, so you will sleep on each side." Then she turned to Jack and Gerard, "You two are married, so you will sleep next to them on the inside. I will sleep in the middle." The four were uneasy with the arrangement, but they knew

Dedee well enough by now to know that once she made her mind up, that was it.

"Larry and Howard, you lie on the bed close to each side, we will sleep in the clothes we have on," she said promptly.

Dedee asked Jack and Gerard to lie down next to Larry and Howard. That left just enough room for Dedee. She blew the candle out and crawled in from the foot of the bed.

"Everybody comfortable?" she asked. When no one said anything, she told them to try to get some sleep.

Jack was uncomfortable. He remembered when he was young, the first time he had stayed overnight at his grandmother's house, and he had had to sleep in his grandmother's bed with her. He had never slept with anyone before, and he was afraid to move lest he wake her or do something to incur her disfavor. He particularly remembered hoping he wouldn't have to go to the bathroom. He felt like that now, only he wasn't lying next to his grandmother, rather he was lying next to a very attractive lady whom he admired. And maybe admired was the wrong word. He knew one thing, and that was that if he hadn't married Mary just before being deployed, things might have been different.

The rain pattered on the roof, and Jack could hear the wind blowing through the trees. He wondered what Mary would think if she could see him. He turned slightly to his side and he could smell Dedee's hair. It wasn't a purchased scent, but it had a natural sweetness to it. His mind whirled. He thought of Mary. He couldn't see her as clearly as before. Then he forced himself to think about the Tiger Moth and his last flight as a pilot. It wasn't pleasant. It was never pleasant, but it occupied his mind and kept it off the woman who lay beside him.

Chapter 6

❧

WHACK. A loud noise echoed up the stairway. Dedee and Jack sat upright in the bed. Dedee had been awake, and evidently so had Jack. The others barely stirred as the two of them got up and rushed downstairs. The wind from the continuing storm had blown the front door open. Fernand shut the door. The jamb was broken, and he had to prop it shut with a chair.

Dedee had imagined the door had been knocked down by the Gestapo or local police. "Thank God, it was only the wind," she said.

Fernand said he had never experienced so much wind before.

Through the early morning light, Dedee could see the tops of the trees bending. "Guess we won't be doing any hiking today," she said.

Elvire announced from the kitchen that she had freshly brewed coffee, and the three of them joined her at the breakfast table, on which she had set bread and jars of homemade elderberry, strawberry, and boysenberry jam. While Jack and Fernand talked about ways to fix the door, Elvire asked Dedee how she had slept. Dedee lied and told her she had slept like a log, but Elvire sensed differently, and suggested that Dedee sleep downstairs with them that night.

Dedee glanced at Jack, "Oh, I think we can manage. The bed is really quite large. We do not want to impose on you more than we already have."

After breakfast, Fernand went to work. The door would be repaired when he returned. Dedee busied herself reviewing everyone's forged papers. She went over each one with a magnifying glass, making sure the forgeries were perfect. She suspected that to get caught on the last leg would be the worst possible outcome. Any of her 'packages' would be thrown in jail and probably denied the rights of captured soldiers guaranteed by the Geneva Convention. The area near the French/Spanish border represented the last chance for authorities to apprehend evaders, and rules and conventions were frequently disregarded.

While Dedee worked, the men whiled away their time playing cards and telling stories. By the third day, she had heard all the stories several times. She prayed for the weather to let up. When Fernand came home from work on the third day, he said he thought the weather would break that night and there was a good chance they could go early in the morning. As soon as the men heard this news, they cheered up. Their excitement about finally reaching freedom was palpable.

That evening, the wind, true to Fernand's forecast, started to die down and the clouds moved off to the east, revealing a nearly full moon. The sleeping arrangements were the same, and Dedee instructed her four men to go to bed early and leave her a space, as she would come up later. Then she went outside with Elvire to check the bicycles. Fernand had arranged to have six delivered and parked at the back of the house. She checked that each one had air in its tires and was otherwise serviceable. They would depart early in the morning, ride through St. Jean de Luz, then on to the small village of Urrugne, where they would meet their new Basque guide, Florentino Goikoetxea.

Several hours after the men had gone to bed, Dedee climbed the steps leading to the bedroom. Her thoughts were bittersweet. She knew this would probably be her last night with her charges. Number one package, Jack, particularly evoked mixed emotions. He represented the first RAF flier she had escorted thus far, and she knew Cresswell would be elated. However, something had happened over the past week. She cared for him. She liked the way he talked about his wife. Jack obviously loved her very much, but she also knew he was attracted to her. Strangely, she enjoyed lying next to him. She even questioned her own reasoning when she said the married men would be next to her in bed.

She opened the bedroom door. Gerard was softly snoring, and Larry and Howard were quiet. She crawled into bed between Jack and Gerard and lay on her back. Even though she suspected Jack was awake, she tried to relax, and pretended to go to sleep. Jack was a bigger man than Gerard, and his weight depressed the soft mattress, causing her to tilt toward him. The night before, she had awakened to find her whole body leaning on Jack's. He was asleep, and she had enjoyed the sensation of his body against hers. She'd permitted herself that enjoyment for several moments before she purposefully moved away.

Dedee tried to concentrate on what might happen the next day. They could encounter mudslides and heavy fog in the higher elevations. German patrols could appear out of nowhere. What would she tell them? The Bidassoa River might be flooded, what would she do? But her thoughts kept coming back to the man beside her. She had always prided herself in her emotional self-control. She had dated men, but nothing ever came of it. Maybe it was because she had always compared suitors to Paul, and no one compared well. Maybe she was just waiting for a guy to sweep her off her feet, but she never gave any man the chance. What would have happened if she had met Jack and he hadn't been married? Would she allow herself? In frustration, she turned on her side, her back to Jack.

Sometime later, toward early morning, she was wakened by the light of the moon shining in her eyes. She still had her back to Jack, but just as before, his weight had caused her to slide toward him. The temperature had dropped, and even though she was fully clothed, she felt chilled. Dedee turned her head and saw that Jack was facing away from her, and without a thought, she rolled over and snuggled next to him. She could smell his clothes, and even though he had not changed in some weeks, she found the odor appealing. The moonlight danced on the back of his now very familiar campaign jacket. She closed her eyes, taking in his warmth. She felt him move and realized he was awake. She didn't pull back. She put her hand on his right side. He covered her hand with his own and squeezed gently. Seconds later, the sound of Elvire's skillet being placed on the stove caused Dedee to pull her hand back. The other three started to rouse, and Dedee slid off the end of the bed and descended the stairs.

"Today's the day," Elvire said to Dedee. "We'll get everybody started with a strong breakfast. Our boys will need it."

Dedee started to cut slices of bread and salami to make sandwiches. "I'm worried about mudslides. The mud will make those rocks up there even more treacherous," she said.

"Florentino will guide you around the mudslides," Elvire said. "He knows those paths up there better than anybody."

"Dear Florentino. What would we do without him? You know, I think he has a bottle of cognac stashed behind every rock up there," Dedee said smiling. "I hear his father was the same way."

The four men came down the stairs and sat around the table. They all had an air of expectancy. They knew the hardest part of their journey was about to begin, but just on the other side of those mountains was freedom, the ultimate goal. They were as ready as they would ever be. After they had eaten, Dedee said it was time to go.

They said goodbye and thanked Elvire, and when they stepped outside, it had started to rain again. It was a light rain, and Elvire told them that these kinds of showers frequently occurred just after major storms. They breathed a collective sigh of relief.

They each selected a bike and Janine led the way. They rode single file through the misty rain. The road was covered with tree limbs and debris from the storm, and Dedee could feel each bump through her seat and handlebars. Janine did not set a fast pace, as if she knew they needed to save their energy for the real challenge ahead: the mountains. Eventually, they came to St. Jean de Luz, where Dedee noticed the local gendarmes were having coffee in a café next to their office. She felt relieved that the storm was keeping them inside and not patrolling for evaders.

Just outside of St. Jean de Luz, the road narrowed until it was little more than a dirt path, and the riding became difficult. The mud bogged the bikers down if they were too slow, and Dedee yelled behind her to keep going. Janine kept the pace steady for the next four miles, until they reached the little village of Urrugne, where they dismounted and walked their bikes up a hill to a small farm owned by Franchia, a friend of Elvire's, who greeted them from her front porch.

As Dedee and her packages approached, they were further greeted by the smell of hot chicken soup, and they forgot that they had eaten only a few hours before, and they were hungry again. Inside, they took off their waterlogged outer clothing, as the kitchen was warm and cozy. The men gathered in a corner, talking about the upcoming climb, while Franchia, Dedee, and Janine shared the latest gossip in French.

Dedee, sensing the men were bored, asked if they would like to listen to the BBC, and not waiting for an answer, reached in front of Jack and flipped on the radio. She didn't acknowledge Jack directly, and didn't intend to. She had decided she couldn't afford the luxury of a personal and pleasurable relationship with Jack. Yielding to her own emotions, if it continued, could endanger her whole mission. In her mind, she tried to erase her feelings toward him.

A short time later, the door opened and a giant of a man entered. His broad shoulders nearly required him to turn sideways to get in the front door. His chiseled face was the color of mahogany and topped with a black beret that sat squarely on top of his head. A tuft of black hair hanging over his forehead gave him a boyish look.

"Florentino!" Both Janine and Dedee squealed and rushed to greet him, Dedee arriving first. His huge arms wrapped around her as if she was his long-lost friend. His rugged face broke into a huge smile as Dedee talked to him in French and he said a few words in Basque. Breaking away from Dedee, he also gave Janine a big hug, then he walked over to the four men and shook hands with each one. His giant hands enveloped Jack's.

The men instantly trusted him. They sensed that if any of them became incapacitated, Florentino would be able to carry him over the mountains.

Florentino Goikoetxea had grown up on a small farm in the Spanish Basque region of the Pyrenees. The Basques were fiercely independent people who fought General Francisco Franco's fascist conquest of Spain in the late 1930s. Their resistance to Franco caused so much trouble for him that he banned their language. As a result, Florentino hated the fascists and any country that supported them. And that included Germany. Florentino did not consider himself Spanish or even French, he was Basque, first and foremost.

Bowls of hot soup were passed around, and while everyone ate, Dedee issued her instructions. She told them to be absolutely silent because their voices could carry long distances in the mountains and patrols might detect them. She told them to walk in single file and to stay as close to the person in front as possible. She said that the trip would take less than twenty-four hours, and the pace would be set by Florentino, who was quick. She told them they would get tired and think they couldn't go on, but she urged them to keep the pace. As she issued her instructions, there was no doubt among the four who the boss was. They all admired her for risking her life to save theirs.

Espadrilles were passed around. These were rope-covered shoes that were flexible and tough, good for the rock climbing ahead. Extra pairs were given to each, along with small backpacks. To be sure each of the escapees had the proper fit for their shoes, Florentino inspected each man carefully. He spoke not a word, but made his wishes known with gestures.

When he was convinced each man was properly equipped, he would touch the end of his thumb to the end of his index finger and nod his head. Franchia had poured six glasses of red wine, and when Florentino was satisfied, he gestured for all to put up a glass.

"Salut," Florentino said and drank the wine in one gulp, then he walked out the door, motioning for the others to follow. As they stepped off the porch, Dedee reminded them to be silent from then on, and she followed Florentino up the path, which wove its way between Franchia's two barns.

Low clouds shrouded their first several miles, then as they gained altitude, they broke out into the clear, starlit sky. The first part of the path was through pine forests, but slowly the way narrowed and steepened as the landscape changed to loose rocks and scree. In the starlight, the men could see that Dedee's backpack was bigger than any of theirs but she kept going at the fast pace Florentino set, never falling more than a step or two behind.

Dedee could hear the men's breathing becoming increasingly labored. She knew that Jack had had no exercise for the last several months, and she suspected the same for the others. She looked back frequently, and one time, when Jack saw her looking, he stuck out his tongue in a gesture of exhaustion. She shook her head and motioned to keep going.

Finally, as they rounded a big boulder that afforded a flat area, Florentino held up his hand. Jack was about thirty steps behind, and the rest were strung out even farther. When they reached the stop, they all collapsed almost on top of each other. Gerard was particularly loud, panting to catch his breath, and Dedee went to him and tried to give him soft encouragement.

Florentino held up ten fingers, meaning the break was to last ten minutes. He opened a bottle of cognac from his pack, took a long, hard pull, then passed it to each of the men.

Jack rubbed his burning thighs, then took a swallow of the cognac. He knew the climb was going to be difficult, and as he looked up the trail, he saw they were nowhere near the top.

Before any of the men were ready, Florentino stood up and motioned for everyone to do likewise. The men had trouble standing, and Dedee knew it would take a couple of minutes for them to get their legs back.

When everyone was ready, Florentino turned and walked past the boulder, beyond which the path was now just a series of steep steps hewn from irregular stone. Some steps were only inches high, but others were several feet, which required the men to use their hands to climb. Jack could only watch in admiration as Dedee easily climbed higher and higher. Her svelte legs just kept moving up and up, as if she had springs. Then she dropped behind and whispered encouraging words to each of her 'packages.' Larry had fallen farther behind than she wanted and she gave him her arm and helped him catch up. He was clearly winded, and he was not too proud to accept her help.

Then Jack slipped on a rock and fell, tearing his trousers and skinning his knees. He moaned from the pain. Dedee was there instantly, helping him up.

"If I can do it, I know you can," she whispered.

Jack said, "How much farther?"

"We're not far from the top," she responded.

"I don't think I can make it," he said.

"When we start down, we use different muscles. You'll be surprised what you can do," she said. "We'll be there before you know it.

"Why don't I believe you?" he said, managing a pained smile.

After another rest, they trudged on, hour after hour. Dedee could feel the slope of the mountain change, and then they were descending. They rounded a corner, and the Bay of Biscay came into view, the gentle curve of the coastline extending all the way to San Sebastián. The rotating coastal searchlight cast eerie shadows as they continued downward, toward the small village of Irun, at the mouth of the Bidassoa River. The men were heartened by the sight. They knew, at long last, freedom was only a few of miles away.

The men knew that because they were descending, the trip was more than halfway over. They made good time. The flexibility of their espadrilles provided good traction over the loose rocks

Then they heard it. Faint at first, but growing in intensity with each step. They were nearing the Bidassoa, and Dedee feared the worst.

"What is that noise?" Jack asked. "Sounds like a speeding freight train."

"It's the river," Dedee said. "And to hear it this far away isn't good."

They continued on, and the river's roar got louder.

When they first saw it, it was obvious no one could get across. The river's source was rainfall in the upper mountains, and normally the span would be only a hundred feet, and the flow would be slow and steady. Now it was raging and ten times as deep as normal. The four men stood, dumbfounded, looking at the torrent, while Dedee and Florentino discussed what they should do.

After several long minutes, Dedee returned to the group and said, "We have to go back."

"Go back where?" Larry asked.

"Back to Franchia's farm," Dedee said.

"But can't we go upstream and cross the nearest bridge?" Jack asked.

"That won't work," Dedee said dismissively.

"Why?" Jack asked, disgust and disappointment in his voice.

"Because the nearest bridge is miles upstream. It's a foot-bridge made of ropes, which might be okay, but there is a guard station at the foot of the bridge and they check everyone going across. They guard the bridge much closer when the water's this high. We must return, gentlemen, back over the mountains. It's our only option. We'll rest here for an hour and have some refreshment. Then we'll begin our return. We'll wait for the river to go down and return in a few days."

The men sat. Dedee could see the deep disappointment in their weary faces. She felt sorry for them, so near to freedom, yet so far. She helped them pull sandwiches from their packs, and she made sure each one had plenty of wine.

Dedee never thought once about her own disappointment, she only cared for her boys, and she knew their best chance at reaching freedom was to go back and try again in a few days, assuming the rain held off.

Chapter 7

❧

Four days later, they were back on the same path, heading over the mountains. Florentino had decided the Bidassoa would still be too deep to cross, so Dedee agreed that they would have to cross well upriver, at the little-used rope footbridge. Despite the risk of being caught by the customs officials that guarded the bridge, the risk of being caught if they did not move was too great.

They planned to cross at night, when they hoped the Spanish carabineros would be sleeping. The guardhouse was located near the footbridge, and afforded the guards a clear view of anyone trying to cross. They departed in the early afternoon so that they would arrive at the bridge well after dark.

The first part of the hike seemed easier than before because it was familiar and the daylight helped them follow Florentino's steps exactly. The four men had confidence in Dedee and their guide, and they felt upbeat about their chances of finally reaching freedom. It was twilight by the time they started to descend, and the view of the Fuenterrabia lighthouse was a welcome sight. It meant they were on the last leg of their journey, they hoped.

Slowly, they descended into the Bidassoa River gorge. They could hear the river's roar, but not as loudly as before. In the darkness now, they followed Florentino as he picked his way along a path that led eventually to the footbridge. Several hours later, they saw it in the distance; however, a light had been installed that shone from the customs guardhouse onto the bridge. When Florentino saw the light, he muttered something in Basque, and everyone knew he wasn't happy.

Several hundred yards before they reached the bridge, Florentino stopped the group. They hid behind some rocks and foliage, and could clearly see two guards standing outside the building, watching for smugglers and evaders. The roar of the river allowed them to speak to each other without the risk of being heard by the Spanish guards.

Florentino gestured and spoke to Dedee, and she related to the four what he was saying. "He says we should wait here and maybe the guards' shift will change," she said.

"What then? How can we possibly get by? Especially with those lights shining on the bridge," said Gerard. "We'll be shot like ducks in a shooting gallery."

Dedee said that Florentino hoped that when the new shift came, they would go to sleep. They had done it before.

Jack looked across to the other side. Here they were again, several hundred feet from freedom, and stuck. He buried his head in his hands and wondered how they could possibly make it. Then a small, brown open car came slowly down the little road to the post. Two guards got out and replaced the two, who rode away. Florentino smiled and gave them an encouraging thumbs-up sign.

The night air was cool and the wind had picked up, blowing upstream. The little bridge swayed back and forth, revealing that some of the slats were missing. Jack couldn't imagine how the flimsy little structure would support anyone's weight. Dedee, maybe, but Florentino? He had to weigh two hundred-fifty pounds.

They waited. The sweat inside the men's clothing caused them to shiver in the cool morning air. The lights went out inside the building, and again, Florentino gave a thumbs-up. It seemed like a dance, and each step was according to their guide's plan. But still, they had their doubts, with the possible exception of Larry.

Maybe it was just that Larry could hide his feelings of doubt better, but it seemed like he always tried to lighten the mood when things got really tough. Once, when they were boarding a train after crossing the Somme, the guard asked to see Larry's papers. Dedee was worried he would find flaws in his forged documents. The guard scrutinized the papers carefully taking a long time. Finally, he gave the papers back and motioned for him to proceed. Larry took the papers, but when he was behind the guard, he gave him a mock salute. Dedee was furious but, later they all had a big laugh.

With freedom so close, they talked about what they would do when they got home. Larry said he would buy a case of the best brandy and ship it to Florentino, then laughingly added he would keep one bottle for himself. Jack said he wanted to get in another Wimpy and bomb the hell out of Berlin.

After several hours, Florentino stood and gestured to them what he wanted them to do. He would go first and he wanted them to wait until he was safely across, then he pointed at Jack, Gerard, Howard, Larry, and Dedee. They would go in that order, and he would signal when each was to start. Through Dedee, he told them to duck down in front of the building, below the window, as they passed, just to be sure no one inside could see them.

Florentino nodded, stepped out into the open, and walked down to the bridge. Using the ropes on each side, he gingerly stepped across, taking large steps when a slat was missing. Just over the bridge, he got down on his hands and knees and crawled under the window, then he got up, passed the door of the post, over the little road, and up an embankment, where he stood and looked back. He motioned for the next.

That was Jack. It was now or never. As he approached the bridge, it looked even flimsier than from afar, but he reasoned if it had held Florentino, he should have no problem. He hesitantly looked up at Florentino, who was motioning for him to come ahead. Jack started. With his first several steps, he felt the give in the ropes. Each time he put his foot on the next slat, the ropes would sag, then as he took the next step, the slat would boost him forward. It was like walking on a springboard. He quickly got the hang of it. Then he came to the first missing slat and his timing was thrown off. His foot missed the next step and he slipped. His leg fell between two slats and he watched one of his espadrilles fall into the water far below. He managed, however, to keep his grip on both of the side ropes and he righted himself and got across. He crawled under the window, then scampered up the hill to join Florentino, who had already motioned for Gerard to start.

Jack immediately reached in his pack and donned another espadrille, silently thanking their guide.

Gerard's low center of gravity was an advantage, and he crossed easily.

Then came Howard, who also fell, but managed to right himself.

Larry was next. He managed the bridge very well. He ducked under the window, but when he passed the door, he pretended to knock. Florentino cursed and motioned for him to come up the hill. Larry scrambled up to the others and showed a big beaming smile.

Florentino grabbed Larry by the front of his coat, and with one hand, hoisted him up in the air like a toy. He cursed and dropped him like a sack. Florentino waited a moment, to be sure no one had awakened, then motioned for Dedee.

She flew across the bridge and scurried up the hill like a feather caught in an updraft.

The elation on Dedee's face said it all. They were in Spain. All she had to do now was put them in a shelter while she hiked to

Renteria to catch a tram to San Sebastián to notify the consulate of her 'packages.'

"Bravo, boys," she said, as Larry picked himself up.

Florentino smiled and shook his head at Larry like the proud father of an overgrown child.

They started walking down an old railroad bed that had years ago been used for mining. The bed led through a tunnel where there was an old water tower held high by a tripod of heavy logs.

"Here is where you will rest until I come back for you. You should be safe here. I'll return early in the morning," Dedee said.

She explained that Gerard would go with her, then he would be on his own to get back to England through Portugal, and Florentino would go back across the mountains to pick up another group of packages.

Dedee embraced Florentino, and when he put his arms around her, she almost disappeared. He shook Jack's hand, pumping it awkwardly. Then he grabbed Larry by his coat and playfully held him up in the air, the way he had back at the bridge. This time he was laughing. He pulled a bottle of cognac out of his pack and passed it around, each time nodding his head as if encouraging them to be sure to take a healthy swallow. When the bottle came back to him, about a quarter of the liquor remained, and he tilted it back and finished it. He said something in Basque, bowed his head to them all, turned, and trudged back the way they had come. Everyone's eyes followed him as he disappeared around a bend.

When Florentino had disappeared over a ridge, Jack asked Gerard if he would contact his wife and tell her he was safe and coming home. They all assumed Gerard would get home before they did because of the higher priority he had as a needed explosives expert. The men said goodbye to Gerard, and Dedee promised to be back by morning, then she and Gerard started walking toward Renteria.

The three remaining evaders climbed up into the water tower. Sure enough, the floor was covered with straw, and there was just enough room for them to lie down. Enough light seeped between the boards of the roof to see. Their voices echoed off the walls if they spoke above a whisper. They had some cheese and bread left in their packs, which they ate, and then relaxed. They were discussing what they would do when they got home when Jack asked, "Larry, why did you knock on the custom official's door?"

"I wanted to ask them if I could use the toilet," he said.

They all had a good laugh and, slowly dozed off, each thinking about finally getting home. Jack's feelings were mixed. While he was excited about finally reaching England and Mary, he worried that he might never see Dedee again.

Dedee returned the next morning and woke the three of them. She seemed distracted, but remained very cordial. She instructed them to follow her to Renteria and told them they would have just enough time there to have a coffee and snack before the tram would arrive to take them to San Sebastián. The walk was pleasant, through lush pastures scattered with cows and sheep.

They were separated by several hundred feet, as Dedee had instructed. She didn't want to take the chance of being noticed as a group, even though the risk was fairly low. The temperature got warmer as they descended toward the village in the early morning sunshine. The men, who were dressed in mountain clothing, felt out of place. An occasional sheep herder would stare and nod as if acknowledging they knew who they were. The local Spanish people shared Dedee's hatred of the Germans and the fascist government of Franco, who supported them.

Even with the threat of the fascists, the Spanish were much more relaxed than the French. Dedee could not believe the contrast in their attitudes and longed for the day her home country would be rid of the scourge of Hitler. With her delivery nearly complete, her mind raced back to her next packages, where they would be, and how she would fight German efforts to close her operation down. She thought of her father and worried about his safety. She had to get back to him and convince him to get out of Belgium, if he hadn't already left.

The beautiful Bay of Biscay was in the distance on their right as they entered the little village. After coffee and a snack, they rode the tram down to San Sebastián. From there, they walked to the consulate. Dedee had warned them that if the consulate was guarded, they would have to wait, but no guards were present and all four walked in at the same time.

When the consulate personnel saw Dedee enter with her three 'packages,' they came rushing to meet them. Their excitement at seeing the evaders' safe return, and knowing that Dedee was to be an extremely valuable asset, was manifest on their faces as they vigorously shook everyone's hands. Even Jack was surprised that his normally stoic countrymen could be so warm and affectionate. Jack's hand was getting sore from all the handshaking and his back was getting sore from being slapped so much. He was relieved when the vice consul asked him into his office.

There, the tone changed.

Jack had to answer questions going all the way back to why their plane had crashed and what their mission had been. The vice consul wanted to know where Jack lived, and about his father and mother. When the questioning was over, the vice consul beamed, "Just had to be sure," he said, again shaking Jack's hand.

"You didn't really think I could be a spy, did you?" Jack asked.

"Of course not, just following protocol. You know, you are the very first RAF flier to be returned," he said.

Dedee watched Jack emerge from the vice consul's office back into the main lobby. The staff was still celebrating the return of the soldiers, and she found her way through them to Jack. She motioned him to the side, where they could speak privately, and reached out for his hands, taking them both in hers.

"I must go," she said looking up at him. "I'm so proud of you."

He squeezed her hands, "How do I thank you for my life?" he asked.

"You don't have to, Jack. Your safe return is my thanks."

They embraced, each holding the other as if neither wanted the moment to end.

"I love you, you know," he whispered in her ear.

"And I love you," she said, dropping her arms and looking down. "Another time, another place—"

She turned away and gathered herself, then looked back up at him, "Please give my best to Mary," she said. "She's a lucky woman."

"I don't know what to say," he said. "I know I will never forget you."

"Have a safe trip home, Jack." Dedee kissed him on the cheek and went to the door, where she stopped briefly and looked back. Then she left.

Chapter 8

NOVEMBER 1941

On a cold Paris morning, Lieutenant Colonel Kurt Lischka, exited the back door of his Mercedes Benz 260D sedan. The address was on the Rue des Saussaies, Gestapo headquarters in France, and his new assignment. Dry leaves crunched under his perfectly shined boots, and he felt the sting of the cold wind on his cheeks. Many members of his new staff waited at the door, heels clicking with nearly unanimous 'Seig heils,' as he approached.

He took his cap off as soon as he was inside, and stared at the others, who got the message and removed their caps as well. They showed him to his new office on the second floor. It was a corner office with four large windows.

Not bothering to look outside, he sat down, and without looking up, said. "Two files please. One, the Jew situation, and two, the Resistance report." When no one moved, he raised his voice and said, "Now."

Lischka had joined the SS in 1933, the year his father died, and his attention to detail and strong antisemitism propelled him rapidly up the SS ranks. His cold, calculated response to Hitler's call for a final solution won him high acclaim. He knew he would soon be receiving quotas from Berlin specifying huge numbers of Jews to be deported, and he knew exactly how he would proceed.

He also knew that this Paris assignment was more than just dealing with the Jews. Hermann Göring was forming his own police force to track down and capture downed RAF pilots. Göring knew the value of trained crew members, if they could evade detection and return to England. The Gestapo did not want to cede this authority to Göring, and they were putting pressure on Lischka to win the war against the Resistance.

The two files he requested were promptly put on his desk. The first, the one that dealt with the Jewish deportation, was a voluminous, bound book, and as Lischka leafed through it, he thought it would take days to read. He put it aside and picked up the second file, concerning the Resistance. It was not nearly as thick. He leafed through to the section marked *Auslandische Evaders.* He lit a cigarette and leaned forward in his chair, adjusting his round, metal-framed bifocals, and as he read, he made notes.

An aide knocked on his door and asked Lischka if he wanted to go out for lunch. Lischka did not so much as look up. His mother had died shortly after he was born and his father raised him to succeed in life. When he was in his sixth year of school, he had received a less than perfect grade in his studies and his father punished him severely. He had quickly learned that studying hard was the key and he never let his father down again.

By late afternoon, he had reached the end of the file and made his last note. The door opened and an aide entered and saluted. The lieutenant colonel smiled to himself. He was sure the entire staff wanted to go home for the day but dared not leave until their new commandant dismissed them. He called them in.

Lischka stood behind his desk, took off his glasses, and in a slow, authoritative voice, started issuing general orders concerning downed enemy fliers.

"I have learned that the Resistance has organized to smuggle enemy crew members of downed aircraft out of France and into

Spain," he said. "Their obvious intention is to return their comrades to Britain through Gibraltar. The Führer has demanded this be stopped. We cannot and will not tolerate this disobedience any longer." He hit the desk with his fist. "We must end it now!" He was almost screaming, and his face had turned red with anger.

The room was stone silent, and Lischka said nothing more for several moments. Then he said in a lower voice, "Here is what we are going to do. There are ten wanted Belgians and a woman in El Murdo prison. These were captured by the Spanish police as they were trying to cross the Bidassoa from western France into Spain. The report says they were guided out of Belgium and through France by a new organization headquartered in Brussels." He pointed to the staff aide on the right, "I want you to go to El Murdo and pick out the most vulnerable of the ten Belgians, the one most likely to talk, and bring him back here for questioning."

He waited. His staff stood at attention in front of him. He looked at the aide, who didn't move.

"Now," he shouted, and the aide saluted and rushed out.

Lischka continued to issue directives aimed at capturing Resistance members who hid or helped escapers and evaders. His directive specifically stated that anyone so caught would be put to death.

The Gestapo had smaller local offices spread out over most of France and Belgium, and Lischka ordered each office to train teams of two or three each, who would imitate downed English crewmen and knock on doors, asking for help. If anyone offered assistance, they would be arrested.

In the following weeks, scores of teams spread out, knocking on doors of suspected sympathizers. Posters were put up in all the train stations and public buildings. Awards were offered for information leading to arrests. At the same time, the Luftwaffe was doing the same thing, concentrating their efforts in areas over which Allied bombers flew.

Chapter 9

⤬

DECEMBER 1941

The black Opel sedan skidded to a stop at 73 Avenue Emile Verhaeren. Nervous eyes peeked through cracks in the curtains of the neighboring houses as two Gestapo agents approached the front door of Paul de Jongh's house and rapped loudly. The cool evening air was still, and the sound traveled up and down the quiet little street like a harbinger of what was to come. Paul had just enough time to hide some fake travel documents before he opened the door.

"Paul de Jongh?" one man said, looking down at a photo in his hand, and then up at Paul.

Without waiting to hear an answer, they pushed him aside and entered the house and climbed the wooden steps to the second floor sitting room, their jackboots made loud hollow sounds that echoed off the houses. They wore long leather coats that hung down past their knees, and with each step, the leather slapped against their boots. As Paul followed them up the steps, he could see from the hair below their caps that they were both blond.

When they entered the dimly lit sitting room overlooking the street, the two agents bowed stiffly to Paul's wife, but neither took off their caps. Without introduction, they started asking staccato questions.

"Where is your daughter, Andrée?" one man asked, reaching into his briefcase and producing a photograph.

"She left home months ago," Paul said, looking up at his interrogator. Paul was shorter than the two agents, and he wore thick glasses that made him appear intellectual. He held the agent's stern gaze. Both agents had cold, ice blue eyes. One wore steel-rimmed glasses that made his eyes appear twice their normal size. While one agent asked questions, the other reviewed notes in a file. Paul noticed the agent's clean, callous-free hands and manicured nails. He was clearly not of the working class, but more likely an upper-class German accustomed to privilege.

"You don't know where your own daughter is?" The other agent asked, incredulous.

"She comes and goes," Paul replied.

"And you, madam? Surely you must know. When did you last see her?" the other agent asked.

Dedee's mother appeared quite controlled even though she was shaking with fear. "I also don't know where Andrée is," she replied. "I do know that she's a nurse and she's probably someplace trying to help people. She is very independent, you know. She may be in Germany, working in a hospital."

The Germans initially smirked at this statement, but when they saw the seeming sincerity in her eyes, they immediately switched to other questions. Dedee's parents held on as the questions continued for over an hour. Was their daughter a spy? When was she last home? Where was she? Who was working with her? The agents finally came to the conclusion that they were not going to get any information regarding Dedee's whereabouts, and they left, saying that if the de Jonghs were lying, they would both be shot.

Paul watched as the Opel drove away. He wiped the sweat off his brow. The Gestapo definitely had Dedee's picture and information, but how they had tied her to the Comet Line, he didn't know, unless someone had been captured and talked, or if they had planted a spy. Then, he thought of Arnold. Maybe they had tortured him into talking. Whatever the case, he knew Dedee could never come home. The Gestapo would be watching. He had to warn her.

Chapter 10

T hree days later, Franchia welcomed Dedee and Florentino back to her farmhouse. The always faithful Florentino had been waiting for Dedee in Rentaria, and they had crossed the mountains together in less than thirteen hours, not stopping once. Rather than being tired from her long journey, Dedee was jubilant. She had been paid by the British for her 'boys' and she was ready to go back to Brussels for the next batch.

After eggs and coffee, Florentino said goodbye and left to pick up the next group, and Dedee bicycled to Elvire's house.

Elvire's face was somber as she welcomed Dedee back. Having a cup of coffee at Elvire's breakfast table, Dedee noticed a troubled look on Elvire's face.

"What's wrong?" Dedee asked.

"The Gestapo visited your father," Elvire said. "And they were looking for you."

"Nonsense," Dedee replied. "I don't believe it."

"That's only the half of it," Elvire said slowly. "You remember the heavy Belgian who couldn't swim when you were taking him across the Somme?"

"Yes."

"Well, a Gestapo agent went to El Murdo prison and took him back to Paris."

"Why on Earth would they do that?" Dedee asked, but she knew the answer before she finished the question.

"They're onto us," Elvire said. "The Belgian will talk, if he hasn't already."

Dedee cradled her head in her hands, trying to think. She had known something like this was bound to happen eventually. She was not worried about herself, but about her father. He had to get out of Belgium, she thought. He could move to Paris and handle the line from there.

Dedee stood. "I must go to Brussels and warn my father," she said.

"Please don't do that," Elvire said. "You will certainly be captured. That is the first place they will expect you."

"I must go. I know Brussels well," Dedee said. "They won't catch me."

Elvire recognized the set of Dedee's jaw. The decision had been made. "When will you go?"

"Are there more parcels ready?" Dedee asked.

"Yes, dozens. Some of our safe houses are overflowing."

"Then I will leave in the morning. We must keep the line moving regardless of the dangers."

On the train to Paris the next morning, Dedee found a window seat in the sparsely occupied car. The air was cool, and the car had been sitting at the station all night, so the seat felt cold when she sat down. She wore a simple skirt, a white blouse, and a heavy sweater that she had borrowed from Fernand. Her white socks and black shoes made her look much younger than she really was. She took a pencil and paper out of her knapsack and started to make notes about things she had to do when she got back to Brussels. With all the pressure from the Gestapo, however, she made sure what she wrote would mean nothing to anyone but her.

The early morning train made its first stop in St Jean de Luz, and many travelers got on, nearly filling her car. A Luftwaffe officer entered Dedee's car and walked down the aisle, looking for a seat. His hair was graying around the temples below his schirmmütze cap. The cap did not have a wire stiffener, and it crumpled in his hand when he took it off.

He stopped by Dedee's seat.

"Ist dieser platz besetzt, junger dame?" *Is this seat taken, young lady?* he asked.

"Non, soyez mon invite," *No, please sit,* Dedee replied, smiling.

"Ah, merci beaucoup," he said, stowing his hat and briefcase under the seat.

He pulled his tunic down to straighten it when he sat. He was nearly six feet tall, and filled his seat completely, and his arms extended very close to hers. His epaulets indicated he was a captain.

"You are French?" he asked.

"Belgian."

"On holiday?"

"Yes. Returning to Paris."

He was quiet for a while, then he said with a soft sigh, "This unfortunate war seems like it will never be over."

"Unfortunate for whom?"

He smiled at her directness. "Unfortunate for everybody, I guess. Many Germans didn't want this war."

"Many Belgians, French, Poles, English, and Americans didn't want this war either," she said.

He looked at her, "I like your spunk, mademoiselle."

Dedee relaxed a little. She thought this soldier was not playing any game with her. He had a wedding ring on, and his tone was not flirtatious in any way.

"Are you a pilot?" she asked.

"Messerschmidt 109s. I'm on my third one. The first two had severe mechanical difficulties," he said with a smile.

"Mechanical difficulties caused by Spitfires?" she asked.

He laughed out loud. "Yes."

He changed the subject. "The Americans are invading Northern Africa. Did you know that?"

"No."

"We have no choice but to occupy Vichy France."

"Why?"

"We can't trust Marshal Petain."

Dedee let the new information sink in. The news of the Germans occupying Vichy France meant that her activities would be scrutinized much more closely. She needed to make sure all of her future evaders had the very best documents.

A French rail employee accompanied by an SS soldier worked their way down the aisle requesting papers. When they came to the captain, the conductor glanced at his uniform, then extended his hand to Dedee. "Documents s'il vous plait."

Dedee was about to give her papers to the man, when the captain pushed them away and said, "Sie its bee mir." *She's with me.*

The conductor looked at the SS soldier, who said in a raised voice, "Dokumente bitte, sir muse see haben!" *Documents, please, we must have them!*

The captain stood up, pushing the conductor away and addressing the soldier, he whispered, "Stick the documents up your arrogant ShutzStaffel ass."

The soldier stared hard at the captain but did not say anything. He made a note in his notebook and the two of them moved on.

"Sorry about that, mademoiselle. The SS represent an ugly side of the German people. Many of us don't like them."

Dedee admired the captain as much as she could any German. He was old school, but she knew he would fight to the death for his country, whether he agreed with its leader or not. For all she knew, he could have been the one that shot down Jack's bomber. They rode together in silence, both of them understanding the vast chasm that separated them. When they reached the Gare de Austerlitz station and they bade each other adieu, Dedee had a feeling they might meet again.

Chapter 11

❧

Dedee cursed her luck as her train pulled into the Brussel-Zuid station nearly two hours late. The delay had been caused by the German 7th Panzer Division returning from the Russian front to assist in the occupation of Vichy France. She had hoped to see Paul at his school, where she did not expect the SS would be looking for her, but he would have left several hours before to be home for dinner. Now she had to take a chance and visit him at home. She figured the later the better, so she took her time walking to there. The night air was very cool and she held her sweater tight around her neck to stave off the brisk wind.

The streetlights were all turned off, but Dedee could navigate well in her old neighborhood with just the ambient light from the sky. When she turned onto her street about two blocks from her house, she stopped to scan the area. The street slanted downward and she could easily see that no cars were parked anywhere near her home. In this area, each house had a small yard in back that butted up against the backyard of the house behind it. A path wove through, separating the backyards. When she came to her block, she crossed over and took the path to her house, and she was happy to see a dim light on in the second-floor window, which meant that Paul was home. She stepped up on the rear porch and knocked softly on the door. Nothing happened inside, so she rapped again, this time a little louder. Then she heard footsteps coming down the stairs. As she waited, she looked around her old porch. A bicycle leaned against the house, the same one she had used years ago. Above it hung her old jump rope, with the handles dangling. She smiled, remembering the rhymes she used to sing when she jumped rope.

I know something
but I won't tell…

She recognized her father's soft footsteps as he came to the door. He looked through a slit in the curtains, and when he saw it was Dedee, he quickly unlocked the door, grabbed her arm, and pulled her in.

In a shocked whisper, he said, "What on Earth are you doing here? Don't you know the Gestapo is looking for you? They come looking almost every day!"

"Oh, Father, you worry too much. There's nobody around."

They embraced and walked up the stairs to the sitting room. The coffee table was scattered with papers. Paul turned out the light and went to the window to check for traffic. Seeing none, he sat next to Dedee and told her how happy he was to see her.

"Mum home?" Dedee asked.

"She's been staying with her sister, who has consumption. It's quite serious, but she keeps hanging on. I guess that's where you get your nursing instincts," he said.

"Paul, I think she is safe, but you must leave Brussels," Dedee said. "I worry about you all the time. I think you should leave Mum with her sister. Nobody suspects her. Move to Paris, where nobody knows you. You could handle our operations from there."

Paul made tea and they talked about the future of their escape line. Paul told her that they had nearly sixty crewmen in various safe houses in Belgium waiting to be escorted, with more being shot down every week. Dedee said she could make a trip every two or three weeks, but they would need additional guides from Paris to the Pyrenees. Paul had several ideas.

Then they heard the sound of a racing car engine, followed immediately by a screech of tires. Paul went to the window and peered out.

"Gestapo! Quickly, the back door!" Paul said.

Dedee rushed to look out the window. Four uniformed Gestapo agents had gotten out of a car. Two were approaching the front door, and two were going around the house to the back, one on each side.

"Goodbye, Father," she said, and she raced downstairs.

A loud rapping on the front door could be heard as the two Gestapo agents met each other in the backyard. They stepped up on the porch. To their left a young girl was jumping rope. Her white socks and plaid skirt keeping the rhythm.

I know something,
But I won't tell.
Three little monkeys
in a peanut shell.
one can read
and one can dance,
and one has a hole
in the seat of his pants.

The agents shone their light on her, but she just continued to skip. Then they heard the agents in front demanding to be let in. The two agents hesitated, then, thinking the young girl was no one important, opened the rear door and rushed inside.

Dedee dropped the rope and disappeared in the night.

Six days later, Dedee was back in San Sebastián with twelve more soldiers. This time they were all RAF, three captains, six gunners, and three navigators. Janine had traveled back to Paris, and they had split the parcels up between them. The weather was good over the mountains and the Bidassoa had its normal flow, which allowed them to cross with much less difficulty.

Cresswell had congratulated her on returning so quickly. She told him her safe houses were overflowing and Paul was moving to Paris, where he could recruit more volunteers to help. Cresswell paid her and asked her what else he could do for her, to which she replied she could handle it. She didn't want any interference from MI9, who were constantly pushing Cresswell to persuade Dedee to accept a radio man, to make communication quicker and easier. Cresswell was sympathetic to Dedee's wishes because he also knew MI9's involvement would impinge on her independence.

Dedee liked Cresswell and trusted him. She knew he was on her side and wanted her to get as many downed fliers out as possible.

"Need more money?" he asked when she was about to leave.

"We always need money, but we can make do with what we have. Many of my people contribute heavily from their own pockets."

"I don't need to tell you to be careful... You know that whenever you solicit another into your organization, you are taking a risk," he said.

Yes, we've had Germans impersonating the RAF, too," she said. "Usually they are dead giveaways." She looked down at the floor as if in deep thought. "I suppose it's only a matter of time."

"We're here for you," was all he could say because he knew she was right.

She opened his office door. "Heard from Jack? He should be home by now... with Mary."

"As a matter of fact, we just got word, he's due to depart Gibraltar on a ship tomorrow morning. He'll be home in a week."

She said goodbye, and left on the tram back to Rentaria, where Florentino would be waiting to cross with her. She scolded herself for thinking about Jack. She had much too much to do and could not allow herself the luxury of such thoughts.

During the next several months, Dedee and her organization delivered seventy-two more downed airmen. Following the German occupation of Vichy, the number of SS dramatically increased, which was especially noticeable between Paris and Bayonne. At each train station, more and more checkpoints had been added, and the inspection of documents increased. Any minor flaw in a document meant detainment.

The Brussels office continued to expand into the countryside, with volunteers constantly watching for British aircraft being forced to land. Their numbers increased so significantly that some fliers were met within minutes of touching down, and quickly shuttled away to safe houses. Guides, who were frequently young girls, would escort them to other safe houses as the evaders made their way to France.

All evaders were supplied with new papers and identities, including addresses. Usually, the new names would be recently deceased Frenchmen, which could fool even the most diligent SS officer. After volunteers produced the forged documents, brave runners delivered them where they were needed.

Chapter 12

MARCH 1942

The man seated on the other side of Kurt Lischka's desk was Josef Schneider. He was dressed in a stylish dark blue pin-striped suit, and his shirt cuffs showed the proper amount of white around his wrists. His right leg, covered by an over-the-calf sock, was crossed over his left, revealing perfectly shined, Italian-made, black wingtips. His thick black hair was combed back with just the right amount of Brylcreem. He had deep-set, dark brown, almost black, eyes amplified by his black eyebrows. He chained smoked American cigarettes.

"You have another job for me?" Schneider asked.

"An easy one, this time. He's an overweight Belgian who was escorted out of Brussels and down to Bayonne by a new group of the Resistance who have organized themselves very well. They continue to operate, but we're having difficulty identifying the mastermind. When we find out, we will erase him. I won't tell you any more, but I need answers now, and I think this Belgian will tell you some things. Especially if you are as persuasive as you usually are."

"Where is he?"

"Locked in the basement."

"Have you fed him?"

"He's been here four days. We have given him no food, and if he closes his eyes to sleep, the guard whips him with a riding crop."

"You're right. Maybe this will be easy. Four days should have loosened him up."

Accompanied by an assistant in a white smock, Schneider entered the cell. The young man was sitting in a chair in the middle of the room with his arms on a table covered in old newspaper. The cell was dark except for a bare lightbulb hanging directly above the table. The Belgian was naked. He looked at Schneider with terror in his eyes.

"Do you know who I am?" Schneider asked.

"Yes," the Belgian answered.

"Then, who am I?"

"You're the guy from Berlin sent to get information from me."

"And did they tell you my name?"

"Schneider."

Schneider pulled up a chair and sat staring at the Belgian.

"This man is my assistant," he said, nodding toward the other man. "He does what I tell him to do and he is very good at it." Schneider could smell fear. He knew this was going to be easy. "Look at me when I talk to you," he continued in a much louder voice. He held his hand out to his assistant, who gave him a sharp file.

The young man couldn't take his eyes off it.

"You will talk, you know. Sooner or later, you will talk and tell me everything you know. We can do it the easy way, and that is for you to talk now, or we can do it the hard way." He twirled the file in his hand.

The young man's hands were palms down on the table and the tension in his arms split the newspaper in half. From somewhere outside, he could hear the sound of a siren. Schneider lit another cigarette, the smoke rising up against the ceiling and bare lightbulb. The siren grew louder. Schneider gave the file back to his assistant and motioned for him to proceed. The assistant grinned and took hold of the young man's fingers, brandishing the file as if to insert it under his nails.

Then the sound of urine falling on the floor under the table. The stream made a snakelike pattern on the uneven concrete as it searched for a drain.

"Her name is Dedee," the prisoner said, pulling his hand away. "She's the one who led us."

"Dedee who?"

"I don't know. Just Dedee."

Schneider motioned to his assistant, who again grabbed his fingers.

"I honestly don't know. But I think she works for her father."

"What's his name?"

"I'm not sure, but I think it's Paul."

"You think it's Paul? Paul who?"

"I don't know. I met them in Brussels."

"Why do you think she works for her father?"

"Dedee cannot be more than sixteen. She's just a kid."

Schneider stood, nodded once more, and left the room.

Schneider was reasonably satisfied with the young man's answers, but he wanted his assistant to make sure.

Chapter 13

JUNE 1942

Paul de Jongh sat at a table in his new apartment on Rue Vaneau in Paris. He had the names of three more crewmen, and he was inspecting forged papers for them to use on the journey from Paris to the Pyrenees. He was worried about Dedee's safety. She had been working tirelessly, and was due to arrive later that day. He was amazed at her physical and mental strength. She would accompany her charges across the mountains, then return almost immediately. While the soldiers she delivered to the British Consulate would be exhausted from just the one-way trip, she would cross back over to the French side and turn around and do it again.

His replacement in Brussels was a man named Jean Griendl, known as Nemo, who had been a friend of Paul's. He had the Brussels operation working well, and he was running ten to fifteen fliers through the network every week. Nemo was from Brussels, and he and his family still lived near there still.

When Dedee arrived, she slumped down in a chair and put her feet up. It was a rare moment of relaxation. Paul brought her a glass of wine, which she eagerly accepted. The apartment was warm and cozy and she appreciated the change from the wet, cold, dreary weather outside.

"I almost didn't recognize you," Paul said, eyeing Dedee's hair.

"Oh, the black? My new disguise. Do I look like an obedient Basque housewife?" she asked, smiling.

"The last thing I would ever think of you as is obedient," Paul said playfully. "I should have spanked you more as a child."

She reached into her purse for a small mirror. "Say hello to 'Aingeru Ekatz," she said primping her hair. Florentino says it means 'angel' storm."

"And very appropriate, I would say," Paul said. "He must think a lot of you."

"We have a great asset in Florentino. He's the best guide we could hope for. I would trust him with my life." Then she changed the subject. "What's happened here, Paul? How is Nemo doing?"

"Brussels has been resurrected. Nemo is doing great. He has a long line of people anxious to help, of course the problem remains: how to be sure they are not spies."

"And Paris?"

"We have great guides, all well vetted, and all anxious to help. Word of our success has made volunteers easy to come by. But we both know that's a double-edged sword. We have so many volunteers, we are having trouble checking them out."

"Cresswell told me, now that many crewmen have been returned, the morale in the RAF has improved dramatically. He said that since the word has spread that there is a good chance of being returned after parachuting into occupied territory, the number of crew claiming to be sick before scheduled missions has shrunk, and the men are now eager to fly each mission."

Paul smiled, "And all because of you, Dedee."

"Us. All because of us, and our volunteers."

Dedee was quiet for a moment, as if searching for words. The 'tick-tock' from the old clock on the mantle sounded like a drumbeat.

"You mean to tell me I must leave, don't you?" Paul said slowly.

"Yes, Paul. And we must move quickly."

Paul had known this was coming, and he was resigned to it. He feared that if he was captured he would not be able to protect her under torture.

"I hate the idea of leaving you," he said.

❧

The train departed Garde de Austerlitz on the sunny afternoon of January 13th, 1943. The entourage included Paul and three crewmen: an RAF pilot and two Americans. Dedee could see her father seated three rows ahead of her. His hair, now totally gray, was visible below his beret, and Dedee realized how he had aged during the past months. He was a dear man, and she was relieved that he would live safely in England for the duration of the war.

Heavy rains drenched the evaders as they made their way from the train to the café in St Jean de Luz where they would meet Elvire. Everyone was soaked to the skin when they entered the café. The three airmen were dressed in peasant clothing and seemed to be enjoying each other's company, seating themselves in a back corner.

Dedee ordered coffee for them, and some for Paul and herself. The proprietor was a friend, and Dedee felt comfortable knowing none of the local police would be out in such a downpour. The hot coffee warmed them all and they settled in to wait for Elvire, as their train had arrived early.

The little bell above the door tinkled and two SS officers came in. Their eyes quickly passed from Paul and Dedee to the three seated in the back. They immediately confronted the soldiers and asked for their papers. None of the three spoke French or German. After the officers had inspected their papers they gave them back and thanked them. Just as they were about to turn around and leave, one German pulled out a cigarette and asked for a light in English. The American reached into his pocket and brought out a box of matches, but before he could strike one, Dedee made a deep, guttural noise and grasped her own throat with both hands. She stood abruptly, and took small steps in a circle, her body straight like a mummy. Then she fell to the floor like a cut sapling, gurgling and twitching. Her hands and arms moved out of sync, her eyelids quivered, then her whole body went rigid.

The Germans moved toward her as if to assist, but when they saw foam spilling from her mouth, one said to the other, "Lass uns hier rauskommen. Schnell!" *Let's get out of here, now!* They both ran out the front door as if Dedee had the plague.

Paul went to a window and watched the SS officers almost running down the street. Dedee got up and brushed off her clothing.

The three airmen just stared at her.

"Boys, when a German asks for a light in English, what should that mean to you?" Paul asked.

The American who had nearly given them away hit the butt of his hand against his head, realizing what he had done. "I almost blew it," he said. "You sure reacted quickly, how did you do that foam trick?"

"The Americans have a water-soluble aspirin pill called 'Alka-Seltzer.' We use it at the hospital sometimes. If you put a pill in your mouth without water, it immediately foams," Dedee said.

Elvire arrived, and they headed for her house, just a short distance away. They left the café owner standing behind the counter, shaking his head. "Une superbe actrice," *A superb actress,* he thought to himself.

The rain was coming down heavier than before and they were soon soaked all over again. Once at her home, Elvira passed out towels, and after some hot soup, she led the three soldiers upstairs, to spend the night.

Fernand joined Elvire, Paul, and Dedee in their sitting room to discuss their pending trip over the mountains. "You will not be able to go," Elvire said to Paul. "The rain has made it almost impossible for you. Dedee and those three soldiers will have a very difficult time, but you, Paul, will not be able. The trek will be much longer and more dangerous because the Bidassoa will be raging at the regular crossing and you will have to hike upstream to the rope bridge."

Paul knew she was right. In the past few years, he had had little exercise other than walking to his school and back, he knew that the trip would be arduous, even in perfect conditions. He had hoped that he and Dedee would be able to go together and say goodbye on the other side, but maybe he could cross with her on her next trip, after the rains stopped.

After a near-sleepless night, Dedee awoke, hearing the rain on the roof. The wind was blowing harder, and visibility outside seemed to be no more than a few hundred feet. Janine had delivered five bicycles for the trip to Franchia's cottage. The three airmen were on edge. They couldn't imagine crossing over in that weather.

Florentino arrived and he too seemed worried. They decided to go to Franchia's house and make their plans from there. Dedee said goodbye to Paul and told him she would be back for him in several weeks. Paul had a bad feeling when he kissed her goodbye. He watched the five of them disappear into the pouring rain.

Florentino led the way. His huge body dwarfed his bicycle. He looked like an adult on a tricycle. The three airmen followed, and Dedee brought up the rear. The pace was slow as they wound their way uphill. Torrents of water cascaded down the paths, leaving mud and debris strewn everywhere. The trip, which would have normally taken about an hour, took twice as long. Dedee thought they were at least safe from prowling patrols.

No one in their right mind would come out in this weather, although she had been proven wrong the night before. She was still bruised from falling on the café floor. She smiled, thinking of the Germans' haste to get out of the café and away from her 'plague.'

Even though Dedee had traveled this route many times, visibility was so low that she only realized they had arrived at Franchia's cottage when Florentino waved to her from the front porch. Soaked to the skin, Dedee and the three airmen left their espadrilles inside the front door and went to the kitchen while Florentino hid the bikes in a shed with the help of a farmhand, Franchia set out warm milk and soup, and they waited for a decision to be made regarding whether or not they would leave that evening.

When Florentino returned to the house, he and Franchia discussed the weather in Basque. Florentino looked worried. When they concluded their conversation, he stood.

"He says you must wait until tomorrow evening to leave," Franchia said.

Dedee knew he was right. She nodded to Florentino, who left to go home.

The three airmen played cards and talked of home over several glasses of wine. Dedee relaxed, knowing her father was safe, at least for now.

Morning broke with a clear sky and promised to be the day the airmen would begin their long hike to freedom. The kitchen smelled of bacon and eggs, and the mood was jovial. Even Dedee was pleased with the weather as she helped Franchia put the food on the table.

Then the sound of a car approaching, and all conversation stopped. One of the Americans took a knife from its sheath and mockingly pointed it at the door. "The Gestapo!" he said, and the other two airmen laughed.

Dedee stood, frowning. The vision of a dark blue kepi passed the window. She quickly motioned for the airmen to go upstairs, but it was too late. The front door burst open and two gendarmes entered with their rifles pointed at those still seated at the table.

"You are under arrest!" one shouted. "Hands above your heads. Turn facing the wall."

Everyone stood with their hands in the air, including Dedee. They had been betrayed.

In that moment of silence, Dedee knew it was over. The coffee pot was boiling, and in the background, she could hear the crow of a rooster. A heavy clumping came from the porch as ten more soldiers entered the kitchen. All five were herded outside while the soldiers conducted a thorough search of the house. Dedee could hear furniture being thrown around and floorboards being pried loose. She felt the mud ooze up through her espadrilles and between her toes. She was dressed in her blue trousers and a light sweater, and the cold morning air chilled her as she tried to figure out what, if anything, she could do.

She eyed the barn, just thirty yards away. She could probably make it before they could shoot her, but what good would that do? She could signal the airmen to rush the two soldiers guarding them, but then what? She decided to wait for a better opportunity.

An hour later, one of the soldiers came out on the porch. "Where is Florentino?" he yelled.

No one answered, and he yelled it again, this time louder, "Where is Florentino?"

Again, no one said a word. An order was given for them to march, and with two soldiers leading the way and two more following, they were forced down the path, with their hands behind their heads.

Dedee glanced back at the farmhouse and saw Franchia looking out the upstairs window. She was weeping.

As they crossed the bridge from Ciboure to St Jean de Luz, five soldiers marched on either side of them, military style. Dedee thought about what had happened, and how they knew about Florentino. Someone had warned the soldiers, but she didn't know who. They were taken to the police bureau, and the

town prison, and each was questioned separately. They were assigned individual cells where they would spend the night.

Meanwhile, word spread of Dedee's capture. When Florentino
found out, he immediately left for San Sebastián, to notify the
British consulate. Elvire spent her time trying to console Paul,
who was shattered.

While she tended to Paul, she started to make plans to rescue
Dedee.

Chapter 14

⌘

L ate on January 16th, Elvire's contacts reported that Dedee had been transferred to the Villa Chagrin prison in Bayonne. This was fortunate because just across the street and within a clear view of the prison was the Bar Gauchy, the same café where Dedee and the three airmen had enjoyed coffee several nights before. The patron of the café, Rene, was a close friend of Elvire, and an avid admirer of Dedee.

Elvire, having already moved Paul to another friend, Jean Dassie's house, could now devote all her time and energy to getting Dedee out of prison.

The first thing she did was to establish her temporary headquarters at Bar Gauchy, where she and the proprietor could keep an eye on the prison in case the Vichy police decided to move Dedee again.

In the kitchen with Rene, she asked if he knew any of the guards who worked at Villa Chagrin. He said there were probably several guards who were not sympathetic to the German cause, and suggested they meet the next day at three o'clock, after he had a chance to meet with them. Elvire enthusiastically agreed.

In the meantime, she hustled around, visiting her loyal friends, soliciting whatever support they could give.

The next day, she met Rene again in the kitchen. With him was a fat Frenchman who wore a uniform with 'Chagrin Prison Guard' on the back. They had obviously been discussing ideas to get Dedee out. Elvire was impressed.

"Madame, we have an idea," Rene said.

"Please tell me," Elvire said.

"You see those soup vats there in the corner?" Rene said pointing to a shelf that contained six enormous vats. "Do you think the young lady could fit inside one?"

Elvire got up and looked at one of the vats closely. "Why almost certainly, but how?"

"Every day, we make soup and fill one of these vats. We haul it into the prison, then take the empty one back. Every day we do that. Our idea is to hide the lady in the empty vat, haul her back here, and 'voila,' she disappears out the back door."

Elvire's eyes got big and she broke out in a broad smile.

"It will not be easy," the guard continued. "We will need several inside to help us. All of them are French, but I would hate to trust them with such an important task."

Elvire thought about trusting other guards to help. She knew the Gestapo was not aware of who Dedee was because if they were, the guard would certainly know about it. The Gestapo would be there immediately if they knew. She concluded there was too much risk. There must be another way. They agreed to meet the next day at the same time.

The next day Elvire, Rene, and Jean Dassie waited in the kitchen for the guard. An hour later, he still hadn't come, and a German Opel drove up in front of the prison. Two Gestapo agents got out of the back while a third SS officer, the driver, stayed with the car. "Dieu, ma chance," *goddamn our luck*, Elvire said under her breath.

"We're too late, maybe," Rene said.

They waited. The SS driver leaned against his car door and lit a cigarette. His holster held a pistol, on which he kept his left hand, smoking with his right. He put his foot on the car door, revealing perfectly shined boots. After about twenty minutes, the prison doors opened, and the two agents appeared with Dedee. As they walked to the car, Elvire could see that Dedee was manacled, though she walked with her chin up. She was dressed in her dark blue mountain-climbing trousers, and still wore her espadrilles. Elvire's heart sank as the car sped away.

"All is lost," was all she could say.

"Not completely," the guard said. "They did this one time before. They take a prisoner to the Bayonne office for questioning. They might bring her back, if they get no information."

Elvire pictured the Gestapo questioning Dedee. She put her face in her hands, and tears came welling out. She couldn't tell Paul this news. She had no idea what he would do, but she was certain it would not be helpful.

Late that night, Jean informed Elvire that Dedee had been returned to Chagrin Prison. They all breathed easier.

The next morning, Elvire met a woman who worked for the Red Cross. Known only as 'Madame X,' she had lost her only son during the blitzkrieg of France, and Elvire knew instantly she could be trusted. Working for the Red Cross, Madame X regularly visited the prisons in the area, including Chagrin.

"Would you be allowed to visit the cell of Aingeru Ekaitz," Elvire asked.

The woman replied that she would, but she was afraid to pass along messages. She knew what the Germans would do to her if she was caught. Rene hid a tiny message, unbeknownst to Madame X, in a small cake, and asked her to deliver it to Dedee. The message said that Paul was in hiding and out of danger and Elvire hoped the news would help Dedee get through the harsh questioning she assumed her friend was experiencing.

Together, Jean, Rene, and Elvire developed a plan for a rescue. None of them had any experience with such matters. They decided that they would use a grappling hook and hoist themselves over the prison wall in the middle of the night. They would extend the hook on a long pole to avoid having to throw it. With little information about the construction of the prison, they thought they would improvise once inside.

They waited several days for a waning moon, and the three set out for the prison. They picked a spot behind a poplar tree that grew between the prison wall and the street. The night was cold, and a harsh wind blew from the north. Elvire could smell the salt air from the bay as they crossed the street, carrying their ropes and hooks. Elvire and Jean wore heavy sweaters, while Rene, who was accustomed to working in a hot kitchen, wore a warm cloak.

When they tried to reach the top of the wall with the grappling hook attached to their pole, they found they had badly miscalculated. The pole only reached two thirds of the way up the wall. They discussed their plight and decided Jean would fetch a long ladder so they could climb up, and then extend the pole from there. Luckily, he found one quickly and leaned it against the wall. Jean, with the grappling hooks in hand, climbed the ladder. He had to climb to the second highest rung for the hooks to reach the top of the wall.

They heard the familiar sound of jackboots marching on the cobblestone street. Elvire, proving she was cool under stress, pulled Rene close and draped his cloak around both of them, as if they were in an embrace. The cloak covered the base of the ladder and the upper part, with Jean stranded precariously, was hidden by the tree. The two soldiers slowed when they saw the two embracing, snickered, and disappeared around a corner. Jean came down the ladder as the two separated.

"There's another wall," Jean said.

"What? Another wall?" Elvira asked.

"If we get over this wall, there's a second wall. We cannot do it," Jean said.

With disgusted disappointment, the three took the ladder and hooks back to the café. They needed a better plan, and quickly. Elvira, bowed but not broken, called for a meeting the next morning.

Elvire thought the best way to form a plan was find someone who was sympathetic to the Resistance and also knew the inside of the prison. Rene knew of another café that was frequented by smugglers, and they were almost always open ways to make money, and daring enough to take big chances. She went to the café and asked the proprietor if he knew of such a person. He suggested a man called "Moon" who happened to be a plumber. A plumber could easily gain access to the prison.

The next morning in the kitchen of Bar Gauchy, Jean said his cousin was the regular plumber for the prison, but because he had three children, he would not be willing to risk being caught, so they agreed the cousin would "get sick" and not come to work. Moon would enter the prison and tell the guard he was subbing for the regular plumber. He would study the interior of the prison, find out in which cell Dedee was located, and determine if a rescue was possible.

The next morning, Moon was accepted as a replacement for the regular plumber, who had called in "sick," as planned. He returned late that afternoon with the news that Dedee had been taken to Fort Duha, a political prison in Bordeaux operated by the Gestapo.

Fernand stopped in at Café Gauchy, looking for Elvire. He needed to talk to her. They went back to a corner table. "One of the airmen who was captured with Dedee has talked," he told her. "Everybody is talking about it at the office. The poor man couldn't take the beatings anymore."

"What did he tell them?" Elvire asked.

"Not so much what he told them, but what he showed them. He took them along the same route they took on the thirteenth."

"You mean they know it was our house where they stayed?"

"Well, not exactly. He didn't show them our house, he showed them another."

"He purposely misled them?" Elvire asked, incredulous.

"It appears that way."

"Thank God."

"It also appears they haven't figured out yet who Dedee really is. But when they do, and I think they will if they have enough time, it'll be all over for her."

"Which means we must get her out immediately."

"How on Earth would we get her out of Fort Duha? It would be impossible."

Fernand smiled, "I was able to overhear my commandant say they were bringing her back to Chagrin tonight."

Moon was back at Villa Chagrin the next morning. A burst waterline on the other side of the prison prevented him from getting near Dedee's cell; however, on the way out, he saw the name 'de Tonga' on the door of the cell he had suspected was Dedee's. He wondered if she had not been returned from Fort Duha after all.

When Moon reported this to Elvire, Jean, and Rene, they all agreed that Dedee must not have returned. Then Elvire got an idea. "What if the airman told the Gestapo Dedee's name was 'de Tonga?' He could have been thinking that if the Gestapo later found out he was lying, he could tell them that he knew it was something similar. 'De Jongh' and 'De Tonga' sound just enough alike that they might believe him."

It was Jean Dassie who spoke up, after a short silence. "You could be right. Yes, I think so, too. The clever airman is walking a tightrope, trying to save his own life while deflecting blame from Dedee at the same time. We must assume Dedee is in the cell marked 'de Tonga.'" They gave instructions to Moon to get as much information on Dedee's cell as possible.

The next morning, Moon told the guard he suspected something was wrong with the stove in the cell marked 'de Tonga.'

The cell was opened, and Moon entered, accompanied by a guard. When he first saw the figure lying on the bed, he thought he was looking at an old woman, but, looking closer, he saw that the woman's hair had been dyed black and the natural brown color growing out looked gray. She was actually a young woman, Dedee de Jongh.

With the guard watching closely, Moon was inspecting the stove, when he saw a ventilator screen mounted into the wall. Without arousing attention, he noted the screen was attached by screws, and could be easily removed. He looked at Dedee, then at the screen. Yes, he thought, she was small enough to fit through. When he left the prison that evening, he looked back, and sure enough, he saw a grille in the wall that had to be the ventilation shaft opening. It opened just above a roof overhang. Dedee could crawl through the shaft, drop down on the roof, then jump into the courtyard. He smiled to himself, thinking he had figured it out.

When Moon related to Elvire what he had found, she became animated with excitement. "We can do it," she said. "Nice work, Moon."

She drew a map on a piece of paper with Moon's help. From Moon's observations, the shaft could not be longer than ten feet or so, which would be no problem for the agile Dedee. They decided they would try the escape on Saturday because the fewest guards were on duty then, and hopefully there wouldn't be one available to accompany Moon when he visited Dedee's cell. As Saturday was only two days away, they tried to think of a way in which they could inform Dedee of the timing of their plan. Moon said that he could do that easily and asked if she understood Spanish, because most of the guards only spoke French. Elvire confirmed that she did.

They made a detailed plan for Dedee's escape, including a fast car that would whisk her to a secret rendezvous point Dedee had told Elvire about, where Florentino would meet her and take her over the mountains to freedom.

The next morning, Moon again entered Dedee's cell, under the pretext that the stove was still faulty. Moon walked into the cell, humming a tune, then he sang some Spanish words just loud enough for Dedee to hear.

"Por la mañana cuando salga el sol,
Me lavare mis manos, mis manos, mis manos..."

In the morning when the sun comes out,
I will wash my hands, my hands, my hands...

When the guard stepped out of the cell briefly, Moon looked at Dedee, who was sitting on the edge of her cot. With a frown on her face, she whispered, "No. Domingo."

The guard immediately returned, and Moon left the cell. Confused, he told the guard he was ill, left the prison, and took a circuitous route to the café across the street. When he entered the kitchen, Elvire greeted him, wondering why he was not at the prison. Moon told them what Dedee had said.

Fernand joined them. "The Gestapo have just arrested Jean Dassie and his wife and daughter. They have been taken to Barritz!"

"Oh my God," Elvire exclaimed. She thought for several moments. "That means the Gestapo know everything. If they arrested Jean and his family, then they know who Dedee really is. We must act now."

A waitress came into the kitchen and whispered to Rene, "Please come and look out the window."

They all rushed to the window in time to see Dedee, now manacled, put into the back of an Opel sedan, accompanied by two Gestapo agents. She was pale, but the determined look on her upturned face gave them confidence. They watched in silence. The bubbling of a giant vat of soup in the kitchen was the only sound.

While Elvire was sadly disappointed, she did not give up. Unafraid, she doggedly contacted as many people as she knew to find out where the Gestapo had taken Dedee. Within hours, Elvire's network produced the answer. She was now imprisoned at Maison Blanche, at Biarritz, another small German prison that Elvire quickly discovered was not well guarded.

Further proving that Elvire's network of friends was extensive, a friend of a friend had a small apartment on the second floor of a building across the street from the new prison.

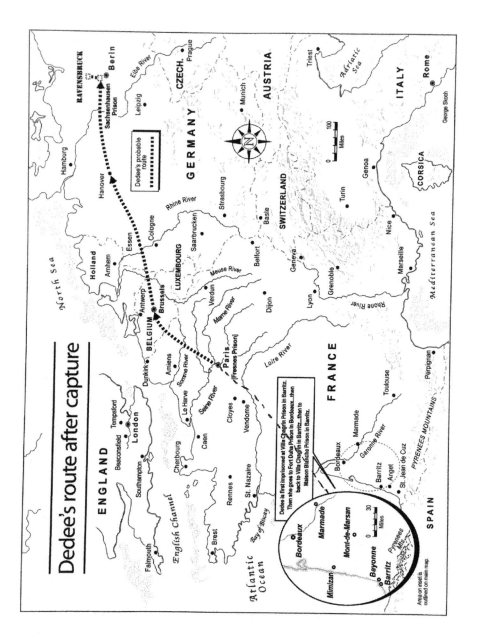

Dedee's route after capture

Chapter 15

❧

LATE JANUARY 1943

The Opel pulled up in from of Maison Blanche Prison. When one of the two Gestapo agents got out and opened the door of the Opel, he glared at Dedee with a hateful sneer, jerking her out of the backseat. "You will talk," he said with an evil grin. "They all do sooner or later."

Dedee glanced at the agent, whose face was directly in front of hers. He smelled of garlic, and he had a front tooth missing. The man looked familiar, but Dedee wasn't sure why. He slammed the door and, together with the other agent took her through the front gate entrance.

During the first four days, Dedee was housed in a small cell with a cot and a bedpan. The cell had a small window high up on the wall that was the only source of light. Like Villa Chagrin, Maison Blanche had a courtyard in the center and at ten o'clock in the morning they could see Dedee's slim figure walking around it. On the second day, Dedee saw a bright light from across the street. She knew it was Elvire. She could always count on her. She was not alone.

No other prisoners were in the courtyard when Dedee walked. Three times a day, the door would open and a guard would give her her meals. The food was very bland, but adequate. The walls were not so thick as to stifle outside noises, however, and she heard the comings and goings of guards and other prisoners.

She knew that her chances of escaping or being released were close to nil. In her own methodical way, she started to form a plan to survive. She knew they had the three soldiers who were captured with her and she suspected they would tell the Gestapo what they knew. It would only be a matter of time. They would eventually end up in a POW camp. Dedee, however, and all her accomplices would be treated as spies and subjected to a different set of rules.

She also knew her segregation in darkness was probably meant to help break her. She suspected she might eventually break down, but she wanted to hold out at least long enough for members of her line to relocate and cover their tracks.

Dedee had never experienced torture before, but she realized it was coming. She started to build a wall between her mind and her body, that would help her survive. Then her mind went back to the sneering Gestapo agent who had driven her to the prison. The toothless smile. Who was he? How did she know him?

Two days later, Dedee heard voices outside her door.

In a staccato German, "What is your name?"

"Harlan Crowe, United States Air Force," came the answer.

"And yours?" the same German asked.

"James Winton, United States Air Force."

Then she heard footsteps as they walked away down the hall. She sat on her cot with her mind reeling. She recognized the voices of the two Americans who had been captured with her. She also recognized the German voice as the one without a front tooth. She thought about what the Americans knew. They both had crashed in Belgium and been escorted to Brussels, then to Paris, and down to Franchia's. They knew a lot. Even though she had standing orders to all her safe houses not to divulge any names, she realized some did anyway. The airmen had not met Paul, however, for which she was thankful. She allowed herself to think about what they knew about her. She was unsure if they knew she was the leader of the line.

That afternoon, Dedee heard voices again outside her door.

"What is your name?" the same German asked.

"Jean Dassie."

Dedee's heart sank. She rushed to the door to hear more.

"What is your name?"

"My name is Dassie, to you, Madam Dassie," she said.

"And yours?"

"Anna Dassie," was a young girl's response.

Dedee again heard footsteps as the group walked away down the hall. Dedee was in near shock. If they had captured the Dassie family, the only way they could have known was either thru the capture of Elvire, Franchia, or possibly the airmen. It couldn't be Elvire, she reasoned, because of the mirror signal earlier. That was Elvire's style. She thought of Franchia. She was very doubtful she would have broken so soon. It had to have been the airmen.

Dedee sat on her cot. What was happening? It was almost like they wanted her to hear whom they had captured. Then she thought about the agent with the missing tooth. She heard the wind blowing hard outside and she could see it was snowing. A rare spring snowfall accompanied by distant thunderclaps. The missing tooth. He wasn't anyone she knew, but the snow rang a bell in her memory.

It rarely snowed in Brussels, and when it did, it would last only a couple of days. When it did snow, it was wet, and snowballs could be formed easily. Dedee remembered having friendly snowball fights with her sister and neighbor friends her age. One year, when she was ten or eleven, the snow had lasted several days, and was over six inches deep. School was cancelled, and she spent the day playing with the other kids on her street. She found that when she made a snowball and laid it in the snow, she could roll it into a bigger ball. Several of these balls put together made a fort-like wall, behind which she could hide as she hurled snowballs. She and her sister made the wall bigger, rounding it on the sides to give them the most protection. Using a stick, she punched holes so she could see without being seen.

An older boy came walking down the street. Dedee recognized him as a bully from another neighborhood. She and her little sister hid behind their wall, armed with a pile of fresh snowballs, should he decide to attack. He walked over to their wall and kicked it down, then laughed at the two girls.

"So much for your little fort," he said. "Girls are so stupid."

When he laughed, Dedee could see he was missing a front tooth. The boy walked away, chuckling.

Dedee and her sister immediately rebuilt their wall. Only this time they made it higher and thicker. The wet snow made it easy to build. That night, the temperature dropped well below freezing, and more snow fell. This time, the snow was unusually light and dry. To Dedee's delight, school was cancelled again, and they played outside. The reconstructed wall, however, had frozen solid, and their supply of snowball ammunition had turned to ice balls. When the toothless boy came down the street that afternoon, Dedee stood above her wall and made a face at him. He came charging over with the same evil grin as the day before.

"Stupid girls, never learn," he said, and he kicked at the wall with all his might. The boy screamed in pain as his foot bounced off the hardened ice. He got up and limped away, moaning.

"Stupid, boys," she'd said mockingly. "They're just are too dumb to learn."

Dedee's thoughts came abruptly back to reality when she heard a key turn in her door. The same agent walked her down the hall. They came to a small room, where he ordered her to sit on a chair in the center. It was the only piece of furniture in the room. He left with that same arrogant sneer on his face.

She sat and waited. She knew she was about to be questioned. She also realized they would be asking the airmen and the Dassies the same questions. How they would answer, she did not know. She steeled herself to admit nothing. If she admitted nothing, her testimony would not conflict with anyone else's, or so she thought. She took deep breaths and tried to relax. Starting with her feet, she worked her way up her body, willing each muscle group to lose its tension. Her concentration was broken by a woman's scream from another part of the prison. It was an agonized wail, long and drawn out. Was it a ruse? She started with her feet again and worked her way up.

Time passed, and Dedee lost track of it. The door opened and a new face entered. A Gestapo agent. Short, with a fat, round face, he stood directly in front of her. He smelled of diesel fumes and she suspected that he had just arrived from outside. He carried a riding crop.

"Your name?" he asked.

"Aingeru Ekaitz."

"No. Your real name."

"Aingeru Ekaitz," she repeated.

"Ah, a Basque name. Are you Basque?"

"Yes."

"Do all Basque women have black hair?"

"Most."

He reached into his case and pulled out a small mirror. She was surprised how easily he found it. He held it up to her so she could see her reflection.

"Then, tell me, mademoiselle, why is your hair not black?"

Dedee looked into the mirror. Her roots had grown over an inch since she had dyed it, and they now looked brownish gray.

She looked back at the agent, and without hesitation said, "These last several weeks have been very difficult. I'm surprised my hair is not pure white."

The agent stood up straight. Then he smiled and broke into a laugh. "Touché, mademoiselle. That was very good."

He walked around her chair, tapping the side of his leg with the crop. Tap, tap, tap. The smile disappeared from his face. Tap, tap tap, he circled again, as if sizing up his prey.

"Your name, please." He repeated.

"Aingeru..."

He lifted his crop high in the air and struck the side of her chair with all the force he could muster. It gave a loud crack that shook her whole body.

She blinked and looked up at him evenly. "Aingeru Ekaitz," she repeated.

The agent stalked out of the room.

Dedee started with her feet all over again.

The agent did not return, and when Dedee was walked back to her cell, she scribbled a message on her wall in very small letters:

Les enfants ont parle et dit tout ce qu'ils savent *The children talked and said everything they know.*

Chapter 16

～∂～

EARLY MARCH 1943

Dedee de Jongh, escorted by two Gestapo guards, exited the train at Garde de Austerlitz, greeted by a cold March wind that easily penetrated her light sweater. One agent led the way and the other followed her closely. She had been ordered to stay close to the one in front. When she had asked where they were taking her, the guards said nothing. The ramp was packed with a rush-hour crowd. The French, all with their heads down and little or no expression on their faces, walked almost mechanically; the epitome of despair and hopelessness. Dedee felt her hatred for the Germans flare in her chest.

That morning, she had been awakened suddenly, well before light, and was told to prepare to leave immediately. It had been nearly ten weeks since her arrest. She dreaded the change. The farther east she went, the closer she would be to Germany, and Germany was the last place she wanted to be. She had held out during her severe interrogations, and her captors had learned very little from her, however, the tone and direction of their questioning indicated to her that they were almost positive she was Andrée de Jongh. But she was also fairly sure that the Gestapo did not know the role Andrée de Jongh had played in the organization to liberate downed airmen.

Dedee kept her head down as they entered the station hall. When they passed the board that listed departure and arrival schedules, they had to weave through German soldiers looking for their gates. The lead guard had to sidestep several times to avoid running into other soldiers. At one point, the guard stepped aside, and Dedee looked up and saw the Luftwaffe captain she had met on her way to Bayonne only months before. When she saw him, he saw her, and plainly recognized her face. When he looked at her guards she saw that he realized she was a prisoner.

He quickly stepped in front of the lead guard, who had no choice but to stop. "Excuse me, Corporal," he said. "Why are you detaining this lady?"

"Because she's a spy," the corporal said smugly. He moved sideways to get by.

"There is some mistake," the Luftwaffe captain said, holding his hand up so they could not get by easily. "Where are you taking her?"

"Fresnes, but it's no business of yours," the corporal said, and he pushed past, and the three of them marched on.

Dedee glanced back at the Luftwaffe captain as they passed. He looked alarmed, following her eyes closely. She noticed a change in his epaulettes. He was now a major.

When the prison guard opened the door of the second-floor cell block at Fresnes Prison, the rush of fetid air almost overwhelmed Dedee. It reeked of vomit, urine, and excrement. The central hallway was covered with dirt and grime, with only a narrow path down the center. Off each side of the hallway were dozens of doors. A rat slinked along the side, seemingly unafraid, as the guard unlocked her cell door. She stood in the doorway, shocked by what she saw. A small lavatory hung from one wall. It was filled with brown, stagnant water. A toilet hung adjacent to the sink, and was smeared with filth. Under the toilet was a used feminine napkin. The bed was a pulldown that hinged up against the wall when not in use. The floor was strewn with old food and bits of garbage.

The guard pushed her hard into the room and slammed the door, which made a hollow, metallic sound. The smell and the sight of her cell overwhelmed her. For the first time she could remember, she did not know what to do. She thought about building her wall, but how would that help her? She could call the guard, but that was unlikely to help. She picked her way on her tiptoes to the bed and pulled it down. It had a thin mattress covered with a dirty piece of fabric that Dedee assumed was a sheet. She turned and walked to the stopped-up sink. It was a stainless steel type, screwed to the wall, and had a gooseneck pipe underneath. Just above the sink was a built-in faucet, and she turned the water knob. Water came out and immediately spilled over the lip of the sink onto the floor. She quickly turned the spigot off. She was not a plumber or a mechanic, but she knew that the gooseneck pipe under the sink must be clogged. She remembered a similar type of sink in the hospital she had worked in just after Dunkirk. When it clogged, a plumber had used a plunger, and the clog had gone through, allowing the pipe to drain. But she didn't have a plunger. What could she do? She reached into the brown water to check the bottom of the sink, but it held no obstruction. She took off one of her espadrilles and gently tapped the gooseneck pipe. She thought if she could vibrate it enough, the clog might pass through. She tapped, and the sound reverberated hollowly. She continued to tap, varying the cadence and force.

After a few minutes, the guard unlocked her door and entered. He had his pistol drawn and he aimed it directly at Dedee. "Stop. No messages!" he yelled.

At that moment, the clog moved, and the water in the sink drained with a whooshing noise. The guard looked at the now empty sink. With the barrel of his Lugar, he pushed the bill of his cap back in wonderment. He holstered his gun and left, shaking his head.

Dedee put her shoe back on. She went back to the bed and wadded up the sheet and washed it in the sink as best she could. Then she started from the corner of the room where her bed was located and, using the sheet, washed the walls, floor and fixtures, pushing all the debris that could not be flushed into the corner by the door. After she finished, she washed it all again.

When she finished, the only light she had was coming through her little window from a light pole in the central courtyard. She lay down on her mattress and realized she had not eaten since the day before. She worried about her father and hoped he had escaped to Spain. She allowed herself to think of Jack. He would surely be back in England. Her mind wandered to their last good-bye. He'd said that he loved her. She found that thoughts of him gave her hope, and even though she was uncomfortable thinking that way about a married man, she allowed herself the luxury.

Chapter 17

EARLY MARCH 1943

E lvire watched the train Dedee was on disappear around a
bend, heading for Paris. She knew Dedee's sudden departure was catastrophic and she wondered if she would ever
see her again. The very thought left her with an overwhelming
emptiness. When she got back to her house, Fernand was just
leaving to go to work, and he told her that Paul was inside.

She stormed into the house and eyed Paul, who was sitting on
a sofa. "What are you doing here?" she said harshly. "You know
you should not be out. You will surely be caught."

Ignoring her question, he asked, "What news do you have of
Dedee?"

Elvire poured a cup of coffee and sat on the sofa with him.

"The news is not good, Paul," she said. "They have taken her
to Paris. I fear the worst."

Paul put his head in his hands and said nothing for a few minutes, then he looked up.

"I'm going to Paris," he finally said. "I'm not going back to
England. I cannot go back knowing that Dedee's work here is
undone. I'll leave as soon as possible."

Elvire recognized Dedee in the the set of Paul's jaw.

"If you must, Paul. You know it will likely be your death, don't you?"

Paul ignored the question. Instead he said, "I think it's quite likely Dedee would have left us a message. She would have wanted us to know what was happening."

"Maybe. But how?"

"I don't know. Maybe a message in her cell."

Elvire stood. "If she did, I know who can find out. Madame X could surely find her empty cell and look for it. I will go see her."

Before she left, she admonished Paul not to go out until dark, then she left to find Madame X.

By the next morning, Paul and Elvire knew the message: Les enfants ont parle et dit tout ce qu'ils savent. *The infants have talked and said everything they know.*

Paul and Elvire were not surprised by this note. They knew sooner or later the airmen would talk. However, now they knew it had happened.

"This is all the more reason why I must go to Paris," Paul said. "If I go, they will think I'm running the organization and not Dedee. Maybe it will save her life."

Elvire reached over and covered Paul's hand with hers. "You are a very brave man, Paul. I wish I had your courage."

With the knowledge that the Gestapo was aware of everything the airmen knew, Elvire set out to warn everyone who had come in contact with the three airmen.

Chapter 18

⟨∂⟩

MID-APRIL 1943

Kurt Lischka walked out of his office into a large room that held dozens of desks, each with a uniformed agent busily working. Six desks were set apart, in a corner, which comprised the section investigating escape activities. All the rest were compiling lists of Jews that Lischka hoped would enable him to meet his quotas for Jewish exportation to internment camps in and around Germany. The quotas came from Himmler himself, and many thought Himmler was being pushed by Hitler for even higher numbers.

But today Lischka was interested in their progress concerning the Resistance activities that enabled downed fliers to evade detection and get back to England. The Special Police of the Luftwaffe had dramatically increased their activity, seeking evaders, and the number of agents working for the Luftwaffe dwarfed Lischka's. He specifically asked about the organization based in Belgium, and recent arrests made near Bayonne. His staff told him they thought the group was actually based in Bayonne and not Belgium, and they had made a huge coup when, through information given by a farmhand, they had arrested many involved.

"Do we know of their leaders?" Lischka asked.

"We have a young woman at the Fresnes Prison who is a person of suspicion," an aide replied.

"A young woman?"

"Yes, a pretty young woman who appears to be French. She claims to be Basque, but she is clearly lying."

Lischka looked at them as a group. "We need answers and we need them now. Use Schneider. If the girl is the ring leader, then we will show them how effective we can be with only a fraction of their resources." He hesitated for a moment. "But don't make a mistake. If we determine the girl to be the leader and we are wrong, we would be laughed at. And, gentlemen, I do not want to be laughed at."

Schneider sat in his office, reviewing the file on the young woman who called herself Aingeru Ekaitz. He filed his fingernails while he read, and dragged on a cigarette which hung from his mouth. The smoke rose up into his face causing him to squint. He was sure from the evidence that the name was not hers. They did know she had been arrested helping evaders to get to Spain. In addition, they knew her group was well organized and seemed to have enough financial support to obtain forged papers. The papers the three airmen had had on them when they were arrested were high-quality forgeries. From the tone of Lischka's aides, they seemed doubtful that this woman was a leader of anything. He put his cigarette out, lit another, and walked down the hall to the room where the young woman waited to be interrogated.

The woman was sitting in a chair facing the door as he entered. She looked at him, but very briefly, as if she only needed a glimpse to be able to size him up completely. She wore odd rope shoes, dark blue pants, a white blouse, and white socks, which made her look deceptively young. She seemed at ease and in total control of herself.

"What is your name?" he asked, standing directly in front of her.

Without looking at him, she said, "Aingeru Ekaitz."

"You're sticking to your story, I see," he said.

She did not answer.

"You will tell me the truth, you know."

"I am determined not to," she said.

"Then, you admit you have not been telling the truth."

"I admit nothing."

"What is your name?"

"Aingeru Ekaitz."

"Are you ready for the torture to begin?"

"I am ready for whatever you want to do."

"You will tell me the truth sooner or later. Why not avoid the pain and tell me what we want to know?"

"I am ready for whatever you want to do." Her voice was firm and even.

Schneider pulled up a chair and sat in front of the woman. He leaned forward so his eyes were even with hers. Her eyes gazed at something slightly to his left. He stared at her. After a few moments, her eyes moved ever so slowly and met his. They held each other's gaze as if the first to blink would lose the contest. Schneider's impression was that if it was a contest, this woman would not lose.

Schneider stood, threw his cigarette butt on the floor and ground it out with his foot, not taking his eyes off the woman. He continued to stare at her almost as if he had made up his mind about her and was looking for a hint of confirmation. After a few moments, he walked out the door, closing it with a slam.

Schneider walked down the hall and up four floors to Lischka's office, and entered unannounced.

"Well?" Lischka asked.

"She's either the coldest, brightest goddamned bitch I've ever come across, or the stupidest. My guess is she's the latter. She looks like a kid. There's no way that person down there, that little kid, that girl, woman, or whatever she is, can be the ring leader of anything. You might want to keep her here for a while and see if she breaks, but my guess is she's not capable of outsmarting our field agents for one day, let alone months."

"You'd better be right, Schneider."

"Have I ever not been right?"

"We'll keep her here and question her on a regular basis. The Luftwaffe wants her to testify at a big trial in Brussels they've got coming up, so after she returns, we'll make sure. If she remains silent, then we'll get rid of her the regular way." Lischka stood and gave Schneider a slight smile. "Now get the hell out of here. I've got work to do."

Chapter 19

APRIL 1943

N early every day, two guards would take Dedee to an interrogation room. It was always the same room, two stories down from the main level. The room was always dark, with one lightbulb shining over a chair in the middle, at which she was seated. The questions were always the same as the Gestapo tried to find inconsistencies in her story. Dedee would build her wall and as the questions were fired at her in fast staccato, she waited and answered slowly.

One day, when the questioning was over and Dedee was returned to her cell, she sat on the bed and began tearing her internal wall down. Slowly, her senses came back to her and she realized she was hungry. She had not eaten in three days. If they planned to starve her to death, she felt they were well on their way.

That evening, her door was unlocked, and a tray was slid in on the floor. The tray contained a bowl of soup, and a cup of water. The soup was a light brown liquid that smelled of rancid bacon fat. She had no spoon, so she slowly drank the lukewarm liquid until only a strange looking glob was left. She didn't have any idea what it was, but she tipped the bowl up and swallowed it, trying not to think about it. Lying on her bed, she tried to banish the interrogation from her mind and focus on something more pleasant. Her thoughts went back to her father, then to Jack. She didn't think of Jack in a sexual way. She remembered his warm touch, his gentle eyes, and that one embrace before they said goodbye. Even though she had been his protector while crossing into Spain, in that moment she felt their roles reverse, and it was she who owed her life to him.

A few days later, the guard unlocked her door and escorted her to the main entrance. She prepared herself for the worst. Two Luftwaffe soldiers stood just inside the front doors in their blue uniforms with black boots up to their knees. When she and the guard approached, they were staring outside through the glass doors. They seemed to be admiring the blue sky and distant view of the Eiffel Tower. When the guard brought Dedee into the entrance area, a Gestapo colonel arrived. He addressed the two Luftwaffe soldiers, telling them that he expected the prisoner to be returned within four days. The two soldiers saluted smartly and Dedee was turned over to them. Then the three walked out the front doors, out the main gates, and down Alle des Thuyas, to a waiting brown Opel sedan. The car headed north toward Gare de Austerlitz, but before it reached the station, they turned onto a small street and stopped in front of a café.

The outdoor tables were crowded with patrons enjoying coffee and the warm morning sunshine. Dedee was amazed by the local citizens, talking and laughing as if the war didn't exist. Two German officers sat at a small table near the street. No one seemed to pay them any heed. Dedee realized that her clandestine activities had conditioned her to be keenly wary of Germans. For those who were trying to live a normal life, the sense of apprehension would not be the same.

The two guards took her inside the café, where there weren't many people, and in a far corner she saw a familiar face, the Luftwaffe major she had last seen at the train station a few days before. He stood and motioned for her to come over. Dedee, not knowing who he was motioning to, looked around to see if he meant someone else. He again motioned, and she walked over to his table, and the major asked her to sit down.

"We meet again," he said, helping her with her chair.

"So we do," she said tersely, not knowing what to expect.

"Allow me to explain myself. As you may have guessed, I care little for the Gestapo. I think, and many others, especially in the Luftwaffe, would agree, that they are a bunch of thugs and killers. They don't represent us and what we stand for."

She looked at him blankly.

"I don't know what you have done to raise such high suspicions with the Gestapo and my own Luftwaffe Special Police, but I do know that if our roles were reversed and I lived under an occupying army, I would resist with every bone in my body."

For the first time, Dedee looked at him with interest. She found herself believing him.

A young couple sat down a few of tables away, and the major lowered his voice. "You are in very deep trouble, madame. If you stay at Fresnes, you will certainly be killed. The Gestapo think you're involved with an escape network, and whether they are right or wrong, they will certainly either starve you or torture you to death."

"I sense you may be right," Dedee said, not offering any information, although she thought he really wasn't looking for it.

"You are being called to a Brussels court to testify regarding your knowledge of a Madam Morelle and…."

Morelle was one of the trusted team in Brussels and when Dedee heard the name, her eyes gave her away.

"So, you do know her? But, again, I do not care about what you have done. I just don't want the Gestapo to crudely end your life…" he looked her in her eyes, "…so soon."

"So, if I die in Fresnes, *c'est la vie*, but what could you do?"

"Not much, I'm afraid. However, I will make sure that you never return to Fresnes. When you finish in Brussels, you will be taken by the Luftwaffe to Germany. Probably to Ravensbrück.

The Paris Gestapo will be furious, but the hell with them. There, your chances of surviving the war are better. Not a lot better, but better."

Dedee had heard of Ravensbrück. It was a women's camp near Berlin. She realized that the major was an honest man who was trying to help her as much as he could. He seemed to feel guilt for some of the actions his country was taking, but the choice between Fresnes and a concentration camp deep in Germany did not sound good. It was like choosing between having an arm or a leg cut off. Neither offered any hope.

The major looked at his watch and stood, "I have to go." He put his hand over hers and said, "I'm sorry I can't help more. Good luck." He motioned to her guards that he was finished.

Dedee was stunned. If they had captured Morelle, then the whole Brussels operation was at risk. All the safe house owners, guides, forgers. Everyone. She felt an emptiness in the pit of her stomach, a premonition of disaster, and she was powerless to stop it.

The guards took her to the car and she got in. She tried to relax so she could think. She started with her feet.

After a short ride to the train station, the guards escorted her to a train bound for Brussels. The two guards sat near the door of a private berth and Dedee sat on the window seat. The rhythm of the train quickly lulled the guards to sleep, and Dedee tried to collect her thoughts. The weather was warm, with sunny skies, and as the train moved through the countryside, she could not help but notice the contrasts. The pastoral views of grazing cows one minute and then a huge fuel dump surrounded by tanks and halftracks the next. A rural school with children playing in a schoolyard, then a platoon of soldiers marching in helmets and shouldered rifles. A small church with an ominous red and black swastika flag blowing in the soft breeze atop the steeple. She was reminded how unnatural it all was, and she again thought about what she was doing and why she was doing it. The German presence was everywhere. She hated them with every ounce of her being, and that hatred stiffened her resolve. She saw little hope of escape, but she would do everything again without hesitation. She thought of Jack and some of the other pilots she had safely delivered back to freedom, to carry on the war. Any one of them could be in the air right then, dropping bombs on Germany. She thought about her father and hoped he was safely in England.

෨෨

The Palace Hotel in downtown Brussels had two floors beneath street level. Dedee's room was a six by six-foot broom closet on the bottom-most floor. She was given time to go to the toilet, then locked into her room with a pail and some bread and cheese. Her guards told her she would testify the next morning. The concrete floor was damp, and she tried to sleep sitting up with her back against the wall. When the door was unlocked in the morning, she felt as if she had been locked up in there for weeks.

The trial was being held in a large banquet room on the second floor. Dedee was escorted to a waiting room just outside, near a central hall. Alone, she tried to think of what she would be asked in the trial of her trusted aide, Morelle. Finally, she decided she could not anticipate the questions she might be asked, so she sat back and waited. After a short time, a man came into the room escorted by a guard. Dedee did not recognize him at first. He was very gaunt and walked unsteadily, requiring the arm of the guard to reach a seat near Dedee. His clothing was in tatters, and welts on his skin could be seen through the tears. When the man saw Dedee, his eyes lit up and he smiled. The guard left them alone.

"Dedee, I thought I would never see you again, are you okay?" The man said.

She turned to look at him more closely and realized he was Nemo, Paul and Dedee's old friend who had taken Paul's place when he moved from Brussels to Paris.

"Oh, my God, Jean, it's you," she said. She went to him and held his hand. "What have they done to you? How long ago were you arrested?"

"Several months," he said, and in almost a whisper he added, "Its been tough." He did not look her in the eye.

She sat next to him and put her arms around him. He was no more than skin and bones and very weak. He smelled of decay and failing health. Nemo had a wife and family and she immediately understood he had not been able to hold out against the obvious torture he had been through.

As she held him, he appeared to be trying to pull away, then he talked, with his head down. "They've got Paul. They raided the Dassie house and took everyone but the youngest child. He didn't have a chance."

"What? I thought he would be in England."

"He didn't go. When they arrested you, he was determined to stay and work. He moved back to Paris, where they caught him."

"Oh, damn him. Damn him. He's the most stubborn man in the world. Damn."

"You mustn't blame him, Dedee. If anything, you should blame me."

Dedee thought of her father and pictured him like Nemo, being tortured. Tears rolled down her cheeks creating streaks on her unwashed face. She had trouble taking a breath. She fought to expand her chest, to take in air.

Nemo stared at the floor, his head starting to shake as he too broke into deep sobs.

"I told them," he said. "I couldn't take it anymore. I told them everything. They even threatened my little girl."

She squeezed him tighter, rocking back and forth. "You can't blame yourself, Jean. You had no choice. Nobody is to blame except the Germans. They caused it all. Certainly not you."

A guard came to get Dedee, but before she left, she told him he could tell them the truth about her. As the guard led her through the large double doors into the trial hall, she looked back at Jean. His head was buried in his hands. She thought she would never see Jean Griendl again.

The large room had three semicircular rows of seats, with each row a foot or so higher than the one in front of it. In the center was a single chair, to which Dedee was escorted. The guard left the room and a major approached. He wore a blue Luftwaffe uniform with the Special Police insignia on the collar boards. The talk among those seated had quieted immediately when Dedee entered the room. The major had blond hair and blue eyes. He approached with a swagger. In his right hand, he held a riding crop. Dedee classified him as just another Aryan supremacist and instantly disliked him.

"What is your name?" he asked, looking at his audience.

"Why am I here?" Dedee retorted, eying him contemptuously.

She no sooner said the words than the major swung his crop across her face. "I ask the questions," he said.

Dedee felt the sting of the blow, but she quickly recovered and glared at him in defiance. She knew he had the upper hand. If she continued to deny who she really was, then her father would be assumed to be the ringleader of her line. The only way to protect her father was for her to tell the truth. That she was the instigator and organizer. It would mean certain death but that thought never entered her mind. She thought of Paul in some dark alley, standing with a rag over his eyes in front of a firing squad, and bullets smashing into him, each one causing his body to flinch as he fell to the ground. She bit her lip.

"What is your name?" he asked again.

"Andrée de Jongh."

"Your father's name?"

"Paul de Jongh."

"Do you know an 'Elvire Morelle' who works for your father?"

"I do know a 'Elvire Morelle,' but she works for me, not my father." Blood dripped from her chin onto her trousers. She could feel the wetness. She heard a few gasps from the onlookers, then the room was deathly quiet. Dedee could feel everyone's eyes on her.

The major smiled. "She works for you?"

"Yes, she works for me, as does Jean Griendl. We call him Nemo."

"Does everyone work for you?" he asked, grinning at his audience. "And I suppose your father works for you, too?"

"Yes, you could say that."

Many in the audience were now smiling as well, but they were nervous smiles.

"Why does everyone work for you?"

"Several years ago, I conceived of an organization that would collect downed fliers out of Belgium and escort them through France and over the Pyrenees to Spain. I solicited friends, and friends of friends who could help."

"Stand up," the major demanded.

Dedee stood, and the major walked around her, looking her up and down. He stopped and placed his hands on his hips and started to laugh. Most of the others in the room also laughed.

Dedee knew they were laughing at the idea that a petite young woman like her, could have outsmarted them for so long. To them, only a man could have engineered such an operation, and they believed they had the ringleader in their custody. Her father. Dedee realized the major still had the upper hand. He didn't believe her. They would remain convinced Paul was their man. She had lost.

Chapter 20

❧

Two days later, Dedee was back at Austerlitz Station, where she noticed huge posters pasted to the walls written in both French and German, all saying the same thing:

Notice: Any male person directly or indirectly help-ing the crew of an enemy aircraft, landed by para-chute, or having affected a forced landing, or as-sisting in their evasion, or hiding or helping them in any way whatever, will be shot immediately.

Women guilty of the same offense will be deported to concentration camps in Germany. Any persons seizing crew members having affected a forced landing or descended by parachute, or who, by their attitude, contribute to their capture, will re-ceive a reward of up to 10,000 Francs. In some special cases, the reward might-be even higher.

This time, the guard led her from the main station, and she had to climb over tracks some distance away. The weather was warm, but the heavy skies, which threatened rain, seemed to make the area darker than it was. She could smell the pungent odor of manure, and realized she was being taken to the stockyard. Dedee was thankful she still had her trusty espadrilles. The footing between sets of tracks was irregular, caused by the large stones on which the rails were laid.

They walked between two sets of cars, and she could hear shouting in German. When they rounded the end of one train, she could see long lines of men and women being loaded onto what looked like cattle cars. The cars were wooden, with sliding doors on the side. German soldiers were herding the people and taking their luggage as they boarded the trains, they tossed the bags and suitcases into enormous piles. Some of the had lightcolored felt stars sewn onto their clothing in front. The passengers made no noise as they slowly moved along, filling up one car then moving to the next. If anyone fell or got behind, a soldier would yell, and others would help to keep the line moving. The soldiers wore regular SS uniforms and helmets, and carried rifles slung over their backs.

Dedee thought there could be nearly a thousand people being herded onto the train. The scene reminded her that since Hitler's rise to power there was a new world order. A world of chaos and hatred in which human life had little or no value and the rule of law was nonexistent. She hated the Germans who had been taken in by such an evil tyrant. She thought about the German citizens who might not like the way people were being treated and how they might be cowering in their houses, afraid to voice their opinions. Or maybe they secretly agreed with Hitler. Either way, she hated them with her entire being and it would be that hatred that would help her survive.

When Dedee reached the end of the line, her escort said something to the nearest guard, who shook his head, looking at Dedee. Her escorting guard left, and although she didn't know who he was or anything about him, she suddenly felt alone in a crowd of total strangers. A middle-aged woman in front of her had two bags, one very large and one smaller. She was having trouble carrying both, and Dedee reached over and took the smaller bag. At first the woman pulled away but when she saw a slight smile from Dedee, she realized Dedee was trying to help and not rob her.

They walked along together. Dedee noticed the woman did not have a star. She had an aquiline nose that gave the impression of strength.

"French?" Dedee asked.

"Rouen," the woman replied. "And you?"

"Rouen is a beautiful city," Dedee said.

The woman nodded as if she knew everyone had secrets. Dedee liked that. She told Dedee her name was Pauline.

When they got to the last rail car, only about twenty were left in line, so when they boarded, the car was less than half loaded. The soldier who helped them board told them they were lucky to have so few in their car. The floor was covered in straw, and the passengers found places to sit around the perimeter. An empty pail sat in the middle of the car. The sides of the car had slits between the wooden boards that afforded a view outside. The inside was smeared with animal feces, and stank of urine, but the straw on the floor was fresh. Dedee sat next to the French woman.

Dedee still wondered if she had done everything she could to save her father. She pictured her father in prison, being tortured, and her heart sank. She knew he would never admit that his daughter was the head of the organization, and the fact that he would not admit it might seal his fate. She saw little hope for her father being freed, and assumed he would be sent to an internment camp.

After several hours, the train started to move, heading northeast. As when she'd left Bayonne weeks before, she knew the closer she came to Germany, the more her chances of escape dwindled. The sensation that she was descending into a deep, dark cave overwhelmed her. In the cave were heavy doors that closed behind her, sealing her off. Each door closed with a clamorous thud like the sound of a steel cell door being slammed shut echoing off the walls.

"Your cathedral in Rouen, Notre Dame, is beautiful," Dedee said trying to break the monotony.

"We were bombed recently, but they missed it, thank heavens," the woman said.

"Allied bombs?"

"Yes. American, I believe. They were after the rail yards. They hit their targets, but a lot of bombs went astray. The damage to the yards was limited."

"You seem to know a lot. Were you involved?"

The woman looked around the rail car to see if anyone was paying attention, then she lowered her voice to a whisper and said, "Yes. I've been helping the SOE."

"The Resistance is strong?"

"Ever since the Germans invaded Russia, the Resistance has welcomed the communists, and has grown to be very strong. I am a member of the FTP and I am a communist," the woman said, frankly.

As the train rolled northeast, Pauline told Dedee much about herself. When she asked about Dedee, however, Dedee remained silent. She had never met a communist she could trust. To Dedee, communists believed that citizens should work for the government and the government should own and control everything. Dedee believed the government's role was only to facilitate citizens to achievement in a lawful environment.

An hour later, the rhythm and sound of the train changed, becoming more hollow, and Dedee looked out to see they were passing over the Somme into Belgium. When she thought of all the evaders she had escorted, who were now fighting the Germans again, she was proud. That would make whatever the Germans had in store for her more bearable. The train slowed to a stop outside of Brussels, and again, they were near a stockyard. Dedee hoped they would be given food and water, but after a long wait, the train started to move again, ever east.

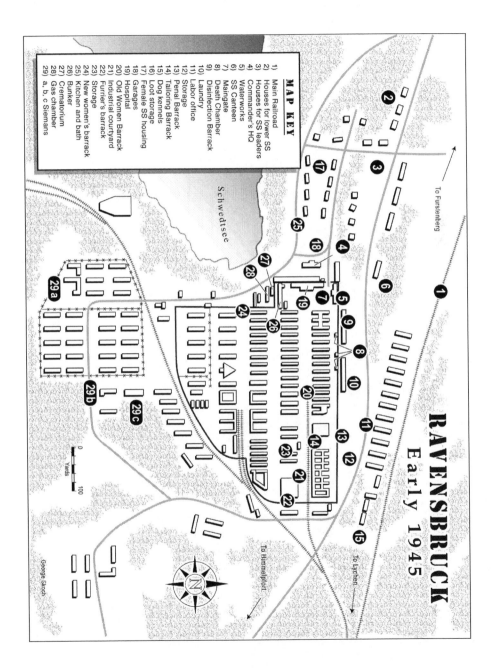

MAP KEY

1) Main Railroad
2) Houses for lower SS
3) Houses for SS leaders
4) Commander's HQ
5) Waterworks
6) SS Canteen
7) Maingate
8) Death Chamber
9) Disinfection Barrack
10) Laundry
11) Labor office
12) Storage
13) Penal Barrack
14) Tailoring Barrack
15) Dog kennels
16) Loot storage
17) Female SS housing
18) Garages
19) Hospital
20) Old Women Barrack
21) Industrial courtyard
22) Furrier's barrack
23) Storage
24) New women's barrack
25) Kitchen and bath
26) Bunker
27) Crematorium
28) Gas chamber
29) a, b, c Siemans

RAVENSBRUCK
Early 1945

Schwedtsee

To Furstenberg
To Himmelpfort.
To Lychen

George Sloch

Chapter 21

❧

On the sixth day after leaving Austerlitz Station, Dedee's train slowed for the final time. All the men on the train had been taken off at Sachsenhausen the day before. Having had no food and little water, the women were weak, and very apprehensive. Above the stench of human waste inside the rail car car, Dedee could smell the familiar damp, fishy odor of a lake, and she was reminded of the summers she'd spent as a teenager at Lake Hazenwinkel, near her home. The train came to a sudden stop, and the waste bucket slid forward and crashed against the forward wall of the car, splashing its contents into the air and soaking four of the prisoners sitting nearby. They hardly blinked.

The moment the train stopped, the ear-piercing strains of *Das Deutschlandlied* blared through the large public-address speakers mounted on tops of telephone poles. The car doors opened and the prisoners were ordered out.

Dedee looked out the open door and her heart sank. In front of each of the car doors, standing about twenty feet away, were uniformed female guards holding the leashes of snarling Alsatian dogs that were straining to get at the prisoners. Behind the female guards were soldiers with their rifles aimed directly at the prisoners. Both the female guards and the soldiers were shouting.

"*Aus! Aus! Aus!*" and "*Schnell! Schnell jetzt! Schnell! Schnell!*"

Some of the women were too weak to step down from the cars, and others did not understand the language. They knew they had to do something quickly but they were not sure what.

The music grew even louder.

"Reihen von fünf!" *rows of five!* the guards bellowed.

In an adjacent car, a woman leaned over to help an older woman who had fallen. She was whipped by a guard. "Keine hilfe!" *no helping!* the guard shouted. The woman continued to attempt to help the woman, and the guard unleashed her dog. The dog sprang, knocked her to the ground, and going for her throat. When the guard yelled again, the dog released its grip.

Dedee, who was fluent in German, whispered to her group to line up in rows of five. A guard came up behind her and swung her crop violently against the small of her back. Recoiling from the pain, Dedee quickly learned, if she was going to help someone, she had better do it covertly.

Because Dedee's last car had fewer occupants, they were able line up in fives well before any of the others. They waited. She looked around. Once again, she felt the sting of the guard's crop across her back. "Augen vorwarts," she yelled *eyes forward.* The guard's voice was high and shrill, full of anger and contempt. Someone up ahead asked for water, and she, too, was beaten with a crop.

Directly in front of Dedee were huge iron gates that formed an opening through the sixteen-foot-high walls.

After what seemed like hours, the prisoners were told to march forward. The music stopped, and only the snarling of the dogs and the shouting of the guards could be heard. A few women were too weak to walk, and they were beaten and left behind, Dedee assumed, to die.

As they walked through the gates that marked the main entry to the prison, Dedee saw a lone woman standing to her left. She was short, a bit stocky, with dark hair tucked under her cap. Her uniform was blue. She eyed each new prisoner, and when Dedee passed her, she felt the woman's eyes linger on her. Dedee kept her eyes straight ahead, her chin up, and she walked steadily, drawing on some of the last energy she had.

Inside the gates was a large central area that lead to long, gray rows of barracks with small windows near the top. Around the inside perimeter was the electric fence with skull-and-cross-bones warning signs every twenty feet.

The guards repeated instructions incessantly: rows of five, hands at sides, hurry, faster, eyes ahead. The prisoners were directed to a large concrete-walled building to the right of the entrance. The guards spoke in German and few of the prisoners understood what they were being told to do, which caused the guards to yell even louder, causing more confusion.

Inside the building was a large square room with shower nozzles mounted on all four walls. In the center, were tables with clothing boxes with sizes marked on each. They were told to take their clothes off. Dedee understood, and immediately undressed. Others followed her lead, but some hesitated to take off their underwear, at which time they would feel the lash of one of the guards. A few stripped to their sanitary straps, then looked around embarrassed, but they were told everything must come off. The clothes were all gathered and amassed in a pile.

While most of the women were embarrassed to be naked, Dedee continued to stare straight ahead, unashamed. Several of the male guards walked in and laughed at the broad assortment of female forms.

When all the new prisoners were naked, and all their belongings including rings and jewelry had been confiscated, six prisoners wearing striped smocks walked in, carrying hand shears.

The head guard, in blue, then arrived to select the women to be shorn. As she passed Dedee, Dedee did not look her in the eye. The guard hesitated moved on.

The prisoners in stripes started with the women's heads, then they asked them to spread their legs and their pubic hair was also shaved off. The male guards became particularly animated during this part of the process. When the women tried to cover themselves, the female guards yelled to keep their hands at their sides.

Dedee assumed they would get striped clothing, the same as the other prisoners, but instead they were issued used clothing from the boxes. The guards distributed clothing to each new prisoner from the boxes that had the size they guessed was close. Dedee was issued a used gaberdine suit skirt, jacket, and light coat, along with a white blouse. When she looked at the clothing and its lining, she saw it was of very high quality, and from that she surmised it had been taken from other prisoners. She was to learn later that the camp had depleted their stock of striped smocks and that all new prisoners would be given confiscated clothing, most of which had been taken from Jewish women.

Next came the identification markers. Each was given a colored felt triangle and a needle and thread. They were instructed to sew the triangles onto the left shoulder of their outer garment. Dedee's color was red, and she later learned that red meant she was a political prisoner. Then they assigned Dedee her prisoner number: 120841. They told her to stitch it into her red triangle. The number would be her permanent identification.

They were ordered outside, into the Appellplatz, where they were counted. This took several hours, as each color was lined up together and counted by the blockfürher, who was the prisoner in charge of the particular block to which a prisoner was assigned. If any one of the groups had a miscount, the counting process had to start all over. When the tallies were finally completed, each blockfürher gave her count to the woman in the blue uniform, who then gave approval.

Each color group then marched to their assigned block. Dedee felt as if she was in a vacuum. Her body was moving, but her mind was blank. Like an animal being moved from pen to pen. Not knowing, just reacting. She was deathly tired and dizzy from lack of food. Dedee noticed Pauline was marching in front of her in the same group. Even though she hardly knew the woman, she felt she was not completely alone. She could hardly call Pauline her friend, but at that moment, she was the only comfort she had in the world.

They marched to the fifth blockhouse on the left. The blockhouses had sleeping areas on each end called blocks. In the middle of each building was an eating area furnished with long tables and benches, a kitchen, and a shower area. Dedee's group was led to the block on the back side of the building. The bunk beds were three high. Dedee was assigned to a middle bunk, on which she found a used toothbrush, a small piece of soap, and a dirty towel. The bed had a mattress of wood chips, and was covered with a thin, checked blanket. Dedee assumed the previous occupant had left suddenly, as the bed looked like it had been slept in recently and the toothbrush was still damp.

The blockova stood in front of the group, and in a sharp, staccato voice, issued the rules of their confinement, in German. Each blockova was also a prisoner and part of the 'kapo' system the Germans used to control the inmates in an efficient manner. This system, which had been proven successful in male prisons, served to 'divide and conquer' the prisoners. By establishing a rivalry between inmates, the energies of the prisoners would be expended on each other and not against their captors. If a chosen 'kapo' or blockova, failed to exert the control that was expected, she would be removed and returned to normal status, at which time the inmates might beat her to death. If a blockova were to treat a prisoner with any form of kindness or favorable treatment, she would be sent to solitary confinement in which many did not survive. The incentive offered to become a kapo was better food and living conditions. Without this system the SS would never have been able to control the huge populations of the camps.

There was never to be any talking between prisoners. Appell was at 5:00 AM sharp. Duty assignments would be made after appell. Beds would be made such that the checked blanket lay exactly flat, with the checks perfectly aligned with the bed boards. Failure to follow the rules exactly meant the prisoner would be put on "report" and the blockova made it clear, being on report would lead to beatings.

After a long list of additional rules and the punishments for breaking them, the blockova led them into the dining room, and each prisoner was given an aluminum cup, fork, spoon, and bowl, with strict instructions that they had to be thoroughly cleaned after each meal. Dedee looked around and wondered what they would use to wash them. They were instructed to take their bowls into the kitchen, where each was given a ladle of soup and a small piece of hard bread.

Dedee sat on a bench next to Pauline and slowly ate her soup. As they ate, no one said a word. Dedee took her time, savoring each spoonful. The soup was a weak broth with vegetables, and as bad as it was, she knew it had to sustain her until morning. Pauline ate ravenously, and Dedee put both her palms on the table and slowly tapped them. Pauline got the message and slowed down.

About this time, the rest of the prisoners in the block entered, having just returned from their daily work duties. None of the women said a word. They just went about getting their food and sitting down. They looked like the walking dead: not feeling, seeing, or hearing. They stared, hollow eyed, at their food, lifting their spoons to their mouths like wind-up toys.

After eating, the new prisoners were instructed to go to bed. They were to completely undress, fold their clothes, and place them at the foot of the bed. Dedee crawled, dead tired, onto her second-level bunk. The past few days had been a blur, and she couldn't exactly remember how long it had been since she left Paris. For the first time, she had doubts if she would survive. The will was there, but did she have the stamina? She thought briefly of her father and fell into a deep sleep.

Chapter 22

⚜

The next morning, the high-pitched blare of sirens pierced the air, rising above the roar of heavy rain hitting the thin roof of the barracks. Dedee sat up so quickly her head hit the wooden base of the bunk above her. Her blockova shouted for the whole block to get up.

"Steige jets aus den bett!" *Get out of bed now!*

The blockova ran up and down the bunk rows shaking those not stirring.

Dedee stepped down to the concrete floor and put on her clothes. The reality of the past few days came swiftly back to her. She could still feel the stinging welts on her back, and her whole body felt like an unimaginably heavy weight. She pulled the blanket up on her bed and carefully aligned the check pattern with the bed sides, as instructed. She thought back to her childhood, when her mother first taught her how to make her bed, and how much she hadn't wanted to do it. Her mother had always stressed the importance of being neat. Her friend Pauline wasn't awake yet, and Dedee, out of sight of the blockova, went over and shook her, telling her to wake up.

"No talking!" The blockova shouted. She stood next to Dedee with her hands on her hips.

The blockova was a short, stocky woman. Dedee guessed she was around fifty years old. The way she talked, Dedee was sure she was German born. She wore a black triangle, indicating she had been a criminal. Dedee was later to learn she had operated a brothel in Berlin. Her blue eyes were piercing, and she seemed to look right through whomever she was talking to. Even though she too was a prisoner, she had an attitude and air of superiority. She moved over to another bunk and said something softly to another prisoner.

Once the blockova moved on, Dedee noticed Pauline did not have her checks lined up on her bed, so she went over and straightened the blanket.

The blockova shouted again, "Kiene unterstutzung! Sie sind auf bericht!" *No assisting! You are on report!* She wrote a note on her clipboard and smiled coldly at Dedee. Dedee had no idea what woman meant by being on report, but finally the sirens stopped, and the whole block was instructed to march out to the appellplatz for appell. In rows of five, with their arms at their sides, they marched out into the pouring rain. A couple of the new prisoners instinctively put their hands up to shield their eyes from the water, and they were promptly either kicked or slapped by the guards.

Within several minutes, the entire prisoner population stood in tight rows of five covering the entire area of the appellplatz. Each blockova was to count her prisoners and report that number to the senior blockova of each barrack. That count was then given to a senior guard, who tallied the count for all the barracks. If at any time, a prisoner fell, stepped out of line, or raised her hands, the whole count had to start over. With so many of the prisoners in poor condition from lack of food, the recount could take a very long time.

As the prisoners were lining up facing the front gates, the head guard, Johanna Lagefeld, surveyed the prisoners from under a large black umbrella. Johanna was the highest ranking female in the German prison system. She believed that most prisoners could be re-educated and converted into productive citizens for the Reich. Her work had drawn the attention of Heinrich Himmler who promoted her over the objections of some of the other prison superintendents, including the present Ravensbrück superintendent who wanted to take a hard line with all prisoners. It was the knowledge that Himmler supported her that enabled her to wield more power. She had a reputation for being fair with all the prisoners with the exception of the Jews.

The rain intensified, and Dedee had difficulty standing. She was so tired and hungry, she felt like she wasn't there. Her mouth felt like it was stuffed with cotton. Her only relief was to lick her lips repeatedly, taking in the moisture from the rain. As the count was restarted for the third time, she thought of her wall and remembered her snow fort from childhood. She tried to concentrate and build the wall again, but she couldn't do it. Her mind was incapable of the concentration required. She tried to steel herself and think of nothing.

The fifth recount worked. Even though another prisoner had fallen during the count, Dedee saw the woman in the blue uniform under the black umbrella nod her head. The prisoners were ordered to march back to their blocks. There they were given a black liquid that was supposed to be coffee, some soup, and a piece of bread. Sitting on the benches, a few of the prisoners who had been there when Dedee arrived whispered to each other when the blockova wasn't looking, but Dedee remained silent. The blockova ate separately and had much more food. When the blockova finished, she approached Dedee, clipboard in hand and a sneer on her face.

"You are on report and are ordered to go immediately to the head guard's office," she said. "There you will learn what happens when you break our rules. Follow me."

Dedee stood and followed the woman to the entrance of the barracks, where the blockova pointed across the lagerstraße to a building just inside the front gate. Dedee marched across the street and knocked on the door. Getting no response, she opened the door and stepped inside.

Just inside the door, a woman was seated behind a small desk. She wore a red triangle on the front of her striped uniform. In front of the desk was sign indicating she was Grete Buber-Neumann. "Are you on report?" she asked.

"Yes," Dedee responded, likewise in German.

"Are you new?"

"Yes. Yesterday."

"Didn't take you long to be on report. Who's your blockova? Oh, let me guess. Grim?"

"Yes, I believe so."

"Wait here," Grete said, motioning her to a chair in the corner.

As Dedee walked to the chair, she passed the open door of Lagerfeld's office and saw her sitting behind her desk, talking to another prisoner. After a while, the prisoner left the office, closing the door behind her. Dedee assumed the head guard would see her soon, but she waited and waited. Grete whispered to Dedee that Lagerfeld was occupied with a major issue and the wait might be long.

Several hours later, Grete went to the office door and whispered to the head guard. "They're coming," and closed the door.

Soon, the front door opened and over thirty prisoners entered. All of them seemed to have injuries to their legs. Some limped and others used crutches. They all gathered around the head guard's office door. Grete said that the oberaufseherin would see them when she had time. A spokeswoman for the group said they would wait.

Time passed, but the head guard did not appear.

Finally, one of the prisoners read a short statement in a loud, distinct voice. "We Polish political prisoners, known as the Rabbits, categorically protest against the experimental operations performed on our previously healthy bodies."

Still, the head guard did not appear, so the spokeswoman repeated the message.

Dedee was astonished. She could see malformations on each of the prisoners: deep hollows in their legs, and legs bent at odd angles. She could not imagine the cause of the wounds. Finally, a group of ten armed SS soldiers entered. They bellowed at the Polish women and ordered them out.

After they left, Grete quickly got up, opened the head guard's door, and said in an urgent voice that she thought the whole group were going to be shot. Lagerfeld hesitated, then picked up the phone and dialed. When the party she called answered, she said, in a very loud voice, "Herr Komandant, do you have permission from Berlin to shoot them?" Then she slammed the phone down.

Later, the head guard appeared at her doorway as if to say something to Grete, and noticed Dedee.

"I forgot you were here," she said. "Please enter." Dedee walked in. As she passed the secretary, Grete wiped her brow with her hand in a gesture of relief.

The sign on the front of the head guard's desk read: *Oberaufseherin Johanna Langerfeld*. "You're on report?" she asked.

"Yes."

"You arrived just yesterday. I saw you get off the train. What's your name?"

"Andrée de Jongh."

"Belgian?"

"Yes."

"French Resistance, correct?"

Dedee had no time to think, but she had to trust her basic instincts. "Yes," she said.

"You're in Grim's block, I know. She was a prostitute in Berlin, and when she got too old to be any good, she took over the whole brothel. She's a good organizer, but not too bright. Can you work?"

When Dedee said that she could, Langerfeld told her to go back to her block. She would take care of it.

⚜

After appell the next morning, Grim called Dedee out and informed her she was part of the group who marched daily to the new Seimenslager.

She had little time to eat before she joined hundreds of other prisoners lined up in rows of five to march out the front gates. The weather had turned cool, a harbinger of fall, but Dedee warmed up quickly, as they were forced to march at a fast pace. She thought back to her mountain climbing days and appreciated that her physical condition was so much better than most of the others. Dedee only knew the word 'Siemenslager' must mean some kind of factory. The march was over a half a mile to a large gate with a circular sign over the top that read: *Siemens & Halske.* A twelve-foot-high electrified fence surrounded a very large one-story building with windows on both sides. The SS guards, who were prodding them to march faster, stayed at the front while the prisoners entered the building. Inside, Dedee was surprised to see rows and rows of overhead lights over hundreds of workstations. The walls were white and the floors a shiny gray, and perfectly clean.

Once inside, Dedee, was told to form a line, elbow-to-elbow with about a dozen other new workers. A factory administrator spoke to them in German in a low, authoritative voice that sounded almost kind. He always started a sentence with 'plez.' "Plez' form a line," "plez hold your hands out." It had been quite a while since anyone had treated her with any courtesy. The administrator, who probably was a foreman, first inspected each women's hands. Two prisoners were rejected and told to leave the line. Then he checked their eyesight, showing each one a typed sheet and asking her to read the small print. Several more were rejected. Two tall women were rejected. In all, almost half were asked to return to their barracks.

Dedee was not rejected. She read the German words precisely, and when the foreman looked at her slender hands and fingers, he nodded approval. She was led to a workstation near the center of the production area, and also near a glassed-in enclosure that held the factory offices. She was told to sit at a station at the end of a long row. There, another prisoner demonstrated her duties. Dedee noticed she had a red triangle, which meant she was a communist. Dedee did not say a word as the prisoner sat down and proceeded to go through the motions that Dedee was soon to learn so well she could have done them in her sleep.

Her station consisted of a small electric motor mounted on a work surface. The motor was operated by a switch that allowed its speed to be controlled by foot pressure. A large coil of thin, red-coated copper wire hung from an apparatus that allowed it to spin freely. Her job was to take a small paper tube, slide it onto the mandrel of the motor, tape the end of the wire to the paper, and press her foot switch so the mandrel would spin and wind the wire into a coil. When the proper amount of wire was wound, she would cut it and remove the coil after taping the wire end onto the coil itself. Then she would start another. The process seemed difficult at first, but Dedee quickly caught on.

Dedee's mentor's German was very broken, and when she showed Dedee a sheet of paper, she pointed to the top number and said, "das pensum," which meant quota, it read one hundred-twenty per hour. *Two per minute.* Dedee thought she might be able to do it. On top of the sheet was the word: *schwingspule* (voice coil). Dedee started to go through the motions of learning how to quicken her pace. After a while, the woman left her on her own. The job required concentration, and Dedee was happy not to have to think.

The one thing she could not get out of her mind, however, was her hunger. There was a constant gnawing in her stomach, which felt as if someone had sucked all the air out of it and it had collapsed into a shrivel. She had to avoid standing suddenly, because if she did, she might faint. Darkness would creep into the sides of her vision, like looking out from deep inside a cave.

A loud buzzer rang, and all the workers went outside, lined up in fives, and marched back to the prison. There, they had only a short time to eat before they were lined up to return to the factory for the afternoon shift. As she walked, it became a habit for her to imagine she was following Jack as they crossed the Pyrenees. She could see him clearly, his long legs stepping over each rock in the path. Then she could smell him. A pleasant, earthy smell that she loved.

The luxury of such thoughts was short lived, however. When Dedee entered her block, Grim was waiting. She slapped Dedee hard across the face, shouting, "You filthy witch. You lied to our head guard. You lied about me, and she gave you a pleasant job. You French are all the same. Sluts. You will say anything. I will fix it for you." She continued to rant and Dedee stepped back after Grim struck her again.

"I said nothing…" Dedee said.

"Shut up," Grim said, and tried to slap her again, but Dedee backed away.

Dedee was shocked by the blockova's violent anger. Grim was red faced, and even though it was very cool, her forehead was beaded with sweat. Dedee could only surmise that Grim was angry because the head guard had not taken her report seriously.

"Did you know I told her you were very tough, but a good blockova?" Dedee asked.

Grim stared at Dedee with hatred in her eyes, but Dedee also saw fear.

"And I told her you had a reputation of being capable of inflicting a lot of pain on the prisoners."

Grim looked around at the other prisoners, who were watching. The hard look in her eyes softened. She may have never received a compliment before, albeit, a perverse one. She took a deep breath, stuck out her chest, and left the block. Dedee hoped she had just made a friend.

The siren blew for appell and the whole block lined up and marched out into the evening air and the appellplatz.

As the weeks passed, Dedee became proficient at winding the voice coils which she had learned were to be used in the new Messerschmitt 252s.

Even though she could wind them faster, she was careful never to exceed the quota. She had noticed some of the other workers who had been there a long time would become shaky from the constant repetitive motion, and when that happened, they would disappear and be replaced by another. Walking back and forth from the prison to the factory three times per day also caused the women to get weaker and fall, at which time they would be beaten by SS guards and if they couldn't get back in line, they too would disappear.

Many of the women whispered their disapproval of those working in the factory. They thought that they should never contribute toward a machine that might be used against the Allied armies. While Dedee agreed with them, she thought that a voice coil that was probably going to be used as part of pilots' headsets was not a particularly serious weapon.

She had been told by the foreman that any attempt to produce defective materials would be met with swift death. In fact, one of the members of her block and been shot when the coils she was making were tested and failed, and were discovered to be purposefully made that way. Dedee remembered, years ago, when her father had explained the function of a loudspeaker. She had always been intrigued by how an electrical signal could be converted into sound, and her father explained that a coil was inserted into an electrical field, and as the current in the coil varied, the coil would move. The coil would be attached to a paper cone, and sound would be generated. The key was that the coil and the field needed to be very close to be efficient, and if the coil was slightly oversize or undersize, the coil would freeze with the friction and not vibrate.

At the factory, each coil she made was checked for continuity and weight, but never for size. She had experimented, making one coil an hour with one extra turn of wire, which would make it very slightly oversize. She then did two coils per hour that way, with no repercussions. She was sure that when full speaker volume would be required, as in the noisy cockpit of a Messerschmitt, the speaker in each headset would work, but it would rub and make a lot of static. Eventually she made all her coils that way. She also figured that once the coils left the factory, they had no traceability back to the individual winder. She felt it was worth the risk, but she could not tell a soul.

The population of the prison began swell. Each day, buses and trains arrived and disgorged more women into the already over-crowded prison. The appells got longer and longer as the prison staff fought to keep control. As the Weimar armies drove east into Russia, a large number of the new prisoners were Russian, and drew a new level of violence and hatred from the SS guards, who regarded Russians as only slightly better than Poles. These women were in deplorable condition. Many of them had been abused and raped by the German forces. Those who got pregnant were allowed to have the babies, and the babies were immediately killed, usually drowned in a bucket of water, many times right in front of the mother.

A heavy snow blanketed the ground as the Siemens workers left the prison to march to the factory. Dedee now wore wooden clogs, which had been distributed to all the prisoners, and the snow built up inside them, forming ice between her feet and the inside of the shoe. By the time she arrived at the factory, she was grateful for its relative warmth. Shortly after she got into the rhythm of the winding, she noticed someone familiar entering the offices located just behind her. It was Grete. Dedee wondered why she wasn't with the head guard.

Throughout the morning, the snow continued to fall, the trees outside bent double in the strong wind, and the lights went out, as did the power to all the winding motors. The prisoners were told to stay at their stations and wait. The windows provided enough light to see, but not enough for them to resume working even if the power was restored. Grete came out of the office as if to check on what had happened, and she noticed Dedee. The foremen and guards were busy trying to figure out how to get the lights back on, so Dedee felt free to talk.

"Why are you here?" she asked.

"Haven't you heard? Oberaufseherin Langerfeld has been fired. She was too lenient on the prisoners. I am now the new secretary for the plant manager."

"Too lenient?"

"Yes. Unless a prisoner was a Jew, they never thought she was tough enough, The SS hated her, and the only thing that kept her here was Himmler, and Suhren finally convinced him to let her go."

Dedee said nothing.

"She saved your life you know," Grete said. "Grim was mad about something. She wanted you in the strafblock where you would have been beaten to death. That was Langerfeld."

"What about the crippled women?" Dedee asked.

"Oh, the Rabbits? Langerfeld saved them. At least they're mostly still alive. Who knows what will happen now that she's gone."

The lights flickered on and off, then stayed off.

"You've lost a lot of weight," Grete said.

"I suppose. The food is not very much."

"You need to get out of here. You've been here longer than most, but eventually you will become too weak and be unable to work." She paused, then added, "They usually shoot the women who can no longer work."

The lights came back on, and when they stayed on, Grete started to go back to her office. Dedee put her hand on Grete's arm. "How do I get out of here?"

The foreman was headed their way. Grete whispered, "Get a job in the revier," and she left.

Chapter 23

∞

PARIS
JANUARY, 1944

The cold, dark January night reflected Kurt Lischka's mood as he entered the front door of his office building on the Rue des Saussaies in Paris. He had spent the last three days in Berlin, listening to his Riechsfüher Himmler issue stern orders for the disposition of the remaining Jews in France. While Lischka shared Himmler's hatred and distrust of Jews, he feared Germany was expending too many of their valuable resources to reach the 'final solution,' which was the total extermination of the Jews. He knew the Eastern Front was not going well, and he thought of the tens of thousands Gestapo personnel who, if deployed in Russia, might make the difference. After all, he thought, what was the big rush? Defeat Russia, then take care of the Jews. Compounding the problem was the vast amount of Reichmarks Himmler's efforts were consuming. That money could be much better spent on the war effort, which included the huge need for additional fortifications in northern France against the inevitable invasion from the West.

From his point of view, the best and most efficient way to deal with the occupied territories was to squash the single thing that was demonstrably contributing to Germany's enemies, the Resistance. Every day, hundreds of bombers were taking off from Britain, heading toward Germany. How many of them had been shot down by the brave German defenses only to survive and return to bomb all over again? He vowed to stop it. After asking for files relating to various Resistance leaders, he sent his staff home for the night, telling them there would be a meeting at nine o'clock the next morning.

The next morning, Lischka's office was filled with smoke as he reviewed with his staff each of the escape organizations that had been formed by the Resistance. These included the Pat O'Leary Line, which operated in Southern France, the Shelburne Line from northern France, and the biggest of all, the Comet Line, which ran from Paris to San Sebastián, Spain.

When the subject of the Comet Line came up, Lischka read from notes he had made the night before. "Do we have the leader in custody?"

"Yes," a staff member said. "We have him here in Paris."

"Are you sure he's the leader?"

Another staff member said, "We are not so sure. His daughter Andrée has been reported by several sources as being the true ringleader. As a matter of fact, she was being held here in Fresnes when she was called by the Luftwaffe to testify in Brussels against another member of the organization, and at that disposition, she claimed to be the leader and organizer."

Lischka stood. "And what did we do about it?"

"The Luftwaffe took her to Germany, and she seems to have disappeared. We think she's in a labor camp, but we don't know which one."

Still standing, Lischka's voice grew loud and demanding. "So, you're telling me we had them both, but now we don't? We had them in our own hands but now we have only one for sure? And they are both still alive?"

The members of the staff did not reply.

"Wherever she is, find her and kill her," he said. "And as for the father, kill him, too." He waited for his order to sink in. After several moments, he turned back to his staff. His face was red, and he lowered his voice nearly to a whisper, "Now, gentlemen, to fail is not an option."

The staff scrambled out, too afraid even to take the time to salute.

Chapter 24

&

Florentino left the consulate in San Sebastián on the late afternoon of July 4, 1944, one month after the invasion of Normandy. This time he had not delivered airmen, rather he had handed a satchel of documents to Michael Cresswell. While he didn't know what kind of documents they were, Elvire had told him they were important for the cause, and that was enough for him. As he understood it, the flow of downed airmen had almost stopped since the invasion because the risk of getting over the mountains was greater than the risk of keeping them in France, so the Allies had decided to keep the airmen in secluded forests in southern France. Everyone was certain France would be liberated within months. By his own count, Florentino had guided more than two hundred RAF and American fliers over the mountains in the past three years.

The spring rains were long over and the sometimes raging Bidassoa was meek as a kitten as he waded across to start his assent up the western side of the mountains. With a bottle of cognac in his backpack, he hoped to be back in Urrugne before morning. The night was clear and the temperature was moderate, perfect conditions for crossing, and he made good time. When he had reached the top, he passed two men he knew. Both were Basque smugglers, carrying heavy backpacks. Florentino asked which path they had taken up and they informed him that their path was clear. The route they had taken, however, was not the fastest, most direct way to Urrugne, and because German patrols seemed to be fewer, he chose the fastest route.

On the last leg of his journey, he rounded a boulder that to him always meant he had made it. He could see the dim lights of the little village straight ahead. He thought about home and realized he was hungry. It wouldn't be long before he was there.

Florentino felt the bullet tear into his right calf before he heard the discharge. A burning, searing pain. He fell to the ground, unable to walk. The rocks echoed with the reports of automatic weapons as he rolled over and over, seeking the safety of nearby trees. In a moment, four Germans stood over him, their guns drawn. He lay on the ground with his eyes closed as the Germans asked him questions. He did not say a word. Finally, they carried him to their car and took him to police headquarters in Hendaye. They treated him roughly, laying him on the floor of the car, but he did not let one sound come out of his mouth.

The police asked him questions in Spanish, French, and Basque, but he did not acknowledge them. They knew he was seriously hurt because he was bleeding and his leg was bent at a very unnatural angle. The Germans took him to a civilian hospital in Bayonne that was run by the Sisters of Charity.

When Florentino was hospitalized, Elvire, true to form, soon learned of it. Through a friend who was an administrator at the hospital, she learned his room number and the names of the other patients in his ward.

Meanwhile, the hospital's doctors set the bones in Florentino's leg, and sewed up the holes left by the bullet, which had gone completely through. Florentino remained mute.

Five days later, Elvire walked boldly into Florentino's ward. She carried a small basket of food and sat on the bed of the patient immediately next to him. The man was French, and Elvire, having learned his name, engaged him in conversation, telling him she was a friend of his father. The Frenchman did not quite understand who Elvire was, but he gladly accepted the food and her good wishes. When she got up to leave, she stole a glance at Florentino, who did not acknowledge her or even open his eyes.

As she passed Florentino's bed, she dropped her bag, and when she leaned over to pick it up, she whispered to him, "Two o'clock."

As she walked out, Florentino broke into a barely noticeable smile.

At exactly two o'clock, three German soldiers marched into Florentino's ward. Two were carrying a gurney

"Where is the Basque spy?" One asked the attending sister.

"We have no spies in this hospital," the nun said.

"Oh, but you do," said the soldier, and as he scanned the ward, his eyes centered on Florentino. "And he's right over there."

They marched to Florentino's bedside and threw back his blanket as if to get him ready to move.

"You cannot move this patient," said the sister. "His leg has not healed."

The soldier looked at the nun with mild contempt, "We have orders, sister. We are moving him to a high security prison. This man is a spy."

The nun moved between the patient and the two soldiers with the gurney with her hands spread as if to protect Florentino. "I beg you not to move this man," she said. "His bones have not healed. You must have mercy."

The mother superior rushed into the ward. "Let us see what 'orders' you have. There must be a mistake."

The third German presented a paper to her that clearly stated their authority, she read it carefully, then said, "You have legal authority to move this man, but you do not have moral authority. You must not move him. He cannot stand it."

"Here's my moral authority," the soldier said, and he turned to Florentino and made a sign of the cross, as if he was blessing him. Then he told the other two soldiers to put him on the gurney, which they did.

During this time, Florentino did not open his eyes or give any indication he could hear what was going on. They carried him out of the ward. All three soldiers marched in the same cadence and their jackboots resonated down the hallways. They put Florentino in the backseat of an old car, and the four of them sped off.

When they had turned a corner and were a safe distance from the hospital, one of the soldiers reached under the seat and pulled out a bottle of cognac, which he put on Florentino's chest. Florentino suddenly came to life, seized the bottle, and drank deeply. The soldier sitting next to him took his hat off and laughed. It was Fernand, and Florentino had recognized him from the first moment they had entered the ward. It was Fernand who had forged the orders that got Florentino out. The three of them wore old, discarded German uniforms, which were readily available in the black market.

They rushed Florentino to a small cottage on the outskirts of Anglet, where he stayed until liberation.

Chapter 25

≈

SPRING 1944

Michael Cresswell sat at the end of a long table in a confer-
ence room in MI9 headquarters in Beaconfield, England.
Also at the table were James Langley, Airey Neave, and
several other MI9 operatives. They were there to discuss ways
in which they could negotiate a trade to gain Andrée de Jongh's
freedom and safe passage to England. Cresswell's insistence that
they come up with a plan to get her out was the force behind the
meeting. He believed the Germans might not have figured out
that she was the head of the Comet Line, and were clinging to
the belief that her father, Paul, was. While he had other business
to attend to in London, this meeting was the real reason he had
taken the time away from his office in Spain. He was haunted by
the scrappy little woman and her ability to organize the com-
plicated issues involved in escorting British and American fliers
out of occupied Europe. Not only were her organizational skills
exceptional, but her bravery and ability to think on her feet were
as well. He knew ahead of time that Langley was against any effort to negotiate a trade, and that Neave was probably on the
fence.

Langley, who was the director of MI9, informally started the meeting. He turned to Cresswell and asked, "Do we know where Dedee is being held?"

"Not exactly," said Cresswell. "We do know she's probably in Germany."

"'Probably' in Germany," Langley repeated. "Not knowing where she is, how would we go forward?"

"We could use an intermediary and work through the Red Cross," said Cresswell. Everyone at the table knew Cresswell was prepared.

"And who might that intermediary be?"

"Count Folke Bernadotte, from Sweden. He has ties to Himmler. If she is in Germany, and I think she is, then she's being held by the SS, and who better to negotiate with than Himmler, the head of the SS?"

Neave jumped in. "He would be perfect, but what do we have that they want? Or, to put it another way, who do we have to trade?"

Again, Cresswell was ready with an answer. "You were right the first time, Airey. It's not who, it's what. Look, Germany is losing in Russia. We all know the Allied invasion in Italy, while taking longer than we'd hoped, will be successful. The Allied invasion of France is inevitable, and many think this war will be over in twelve months. The Germans have to know that, and of all people, Himmler will want to hedge his bets."

"Hedge his bets?" Langley asked.

Cresswell twirled his pen in his fingers. "We trade safe passage of Heinrich Himmler from Germany to South America, or someplace else, for Dedee's release."

The room went stone silent. All were aghast.

"Never fly," Langley said. "No way. I doubt anyone would approve a trade for Himmler, even if we were trading the Vice President."

Cresswell was prepared. "How about Himmler's family?" he asked.

All were silent.

Finally, Langley spoke up and said, "Cresswell, you've got balls. I like that. But even if I agreed with you, this would have to go up the ladder... Way up the ladder."

The meeting was adjourned with Langley saying he would look into it.

Chapter 26

❧

RAVENSBRÜCK PRISON
SPRING, 1944

On Sundays, work was over when the prisoners returned
for lunch. Rules were relaxed somewhat the rest of the
day, and prisoners inside each block could mingle and
talk freely. On Sunday afternoons, the guards had the rest of the
day off.

Because she was fluent in German and French, Dedee helped
some of the women learn German. She would sit on the edge
of her bunk while others gathered around, and repeat various
words and clauses in French and then the German equivalents.
It was an effective way to pass the time, and also helped those
who could not understand German, because the blockovas all
demanded that only German be spoken inside the prison walls.
Failure to do so usually put a prisoner 'on report.'

Her most ardent student was Pauline, who had been on a
daily work crew that left each morning and marched outside the
gates to a nearby forest, where they were forced to chop and split
wood all day. The work was taking a toll on Pauline. She had lost
a lot of weight. Her face sagged and her shoulders were so much

thinner than before. Dedee wondered how long she could continue to do that kind of heavy work.

Pauline was an information hound. She seemed to have a flair for finding things out and putting two and two together. When Dedee told her what Grete had said about finding a job at the revier, Pauline understood her logic. Her theory was the Germans needed healthy workers to meet the increasing demand in their factories. When Dedee asked why they were killing so many prisoners, Pauline rightfully pointed out that they were only killing the prisoners who couldn't work. She also said that even some prisoners who had trouble walking and were bedridden were still used to knit socks for the army. She also argued that the old head doctor in the revier was gone, and the new one, Doctor Treite, was different. He wanted patients to get better so they could go back to work.

Several weeks later, during the evening appell, a young man in a white coat stood next to the head guard and yelled through a megaphone that he was Dr. Treite and he was looking for doctors and nurses, or anyone with hospital experience. No one immediately volunteered, but that evening Pauline told Dedee she was going to and she thought Dedee should, as well. They informed Grim, who later instructed both to report to the revier during their lunch period the next day. Dedee was hired because of her prior nursing experience in Belgium; Pauline, however, was not.

On the walk back from the Siemenslager at noon the next day, Dedee heard an unfamiliar roar overhead. The sun shone brightly and the sky was clear. She stole a glance up, as did almost everyone else in the line. The guards yelled at the prisoners to keep their eyes forward and hands down, but, everyone saw them. Hundreds and hundreds of Allied bombers heading south, toward Berlin. For the first time in months, Dedee felt hope and even a little joy. She wondered if Jack might be up there in one of those bombers.

By the time she was back in her block and drinking the tepid black fluid they called coffee, she could faintly hear the bombs exploding. She glanced over at Grim. For the first time, the blockova was laughing. It wasn't until then that Dedee realized she had lost a couple of her front teeth. Dedee guessed she had been cruelly abused when she was young.

Dedee drank the 'coffee' and quickly ate the watery soup, and asked permission to go to the revier, which was granted.

When Dedee entered the revier, she felt as if she had entered another world. Doctors wore white coats, nurses wore freshly ironed gray dresses, the floors were perfectly clean, and the beds had real white sheets. Pauline had been correct, the hospital really seemed to be trying to make prisoners better so they could go back to work, which was a step up from not trying to make them better at all.

She met the head nurse, Oberschwester Marschall, who asked for her qualifications, and after a short conversation, assigned her to help change bandages. When Dedee saw the supplies of towels, sheets, medicines, and bandages, she was amazed.

An advantage of her new job was that she was required to shower before starting work every morning. Dedee was elated to be clean, though the stark difference between the inside of the hospital and the rest of the camp made her feel uneasy. Granted, the revier was helping prisoners regain their health, but with a sadistic ulterior motive.

On Dedee's first full day, she was allowed to walk freely from ward to ward. Between two of the wards was a small room where doctors had coffee. When she passed the room, the aroma of the coffee swept over her like the embrace of a long-lost friend. She stopped. The sign on the door said 'Nur Arzte' *Doctors Only.*

Dedee saw real cream and sugar beside the coffee urn. She looked up and down the hall and saw no one. She hesitated, then, thinking better of it, she went on to the next ward. The staff nurses checked on her work periodically, and when Dedee heard no comments, she assumed they were satisfied. She was also satisfied helping the prisoners, some of whom would whimper when she cleaned their wounds with antiseptic. Many of the wounds she treated were inflicted by the SS guards. Dedee noticed that prisoners who had diseases that might be chronic or take a long time to heal, would disappear. She could only assume they were shot.

The camp had what the prisoners referred to as a 'shooting alley.' It was located between a garage and the camp bunker where solitary confinement and torture were carried out. The 'alley' was about sixty feet long. Dedee had never seen it, but she had seen prisoners marched in that direction. A sight always followed shortly by gunshots. All the prisoners knew it was there. The shootings would take place in the early mornings, before Triete came to the hospital. Some assumed it was his job to certify that the prisoners were dead.

The flow of Russian prisoners had ceased, and new arrivals were now mostly from Norway, Denmark, or the Balkans. Some were brought from other concentration camps as the Russians neared the German border. As a result, conditions inside the blocks became more crowded. Two prisoners now occupied each bunk. Dedee shared hers with Pauline.

Pauline continued wood chopping duty. Sometimes she would be too tired to eat, and standing for a long appell was almost impossible for her. Dedee would bring Pauline's rations to their bed, and even gave her some of her own.

Pauline was also developing a deep cough that would shake the whole bunk in the night.

When Dedee arrived early one morning, the general mood in the revier was gloomy. The German nurses and doctors whispered to one another, but would stop when Dedee entered the room. They had heard the Allies were landing in Normandy.

Dedee pushed a small cart from ward to ward carrying bandages and cotton swabs, and as she passed the coffee room that day, she stopped to inhale the wonderful aroma. She looked up and down the hallway and saw no one, and on the spur of the moment, she went in and put three sugar cubes in her pocket.

She felt the familiar crystalline texture of the cubes, and her mouth watered, but she planned to give them to Pauline.

When she turned to leave the room, Doctor Triete was standing in the doorway. He looked at her not with a threatening 'I caught you' look, but with a strange, sad expression.

Dedee turned to put the sugar back.

"No need to put them back," he said. "But why do you want them?"

Quickly recovering, Dedee said, "My friend works splitting wood every day, and every day she gets weaker and weaker. She has a terrible cough, too. I thought some sugar might help her."

"If she is sick, why don't you have her come to the revier?'

Dedee could see that the doctor was not trying to trap her, so she told him the truth.

"Doctor, I believe my friend may have tuberculosis. If she comes here and the treatment fails, I do not want her to go missing."

"Go missing...?"

"Yes."

After a few moments of thought, Triete turned to walk out, and as he passed through the doorway, he said, "Carry on."

Dedee was stunned, but quickly recovered. During the following months, she smuggled not only sugar cubes, but supplies, soaps, and medicines back to her block. She felt she had a certain privilege. She was never overt, but each day, she brought something back. In addition, when cleaning the wards in the evening, she saw various German newspapers lying around. She did not take them, rather she scanned them for pertinent information about the war, and on Sunday afternoons, the whole block would gather around, and Dedee would tell them what she had read.

One Sunday in June, she told them that the Western Allied Forces had invaded France. Even Grim was elated. The whole block cheered. The prisoners finally had a real reason for hope. With the Russians pushing the Germans from the east and the

Allies pushing from the west, they thought the end of the war might be only months away.

The SS had started to change their philosophy. They realized that the war was probably lost. Their need for workers dwindled, as did their attention to keeping them alive. More and more new prisoners came through the front gates daily, now from Hungary and Czechoslovakia. The prison was so crowded that many of those new arrivals were never registered, but instead were immediately shot and incinerated in a newly constructed crematory.

Chapter 27

◈

SAN SEBASTIÁN, SPAIN
AUGUST 1944

Michael Cresswell's assistant entered his office with a copy of a wire sent from London. He handed it to Cresswell and noted it was from MI9.

We have discussed your proposal regarding the pardon of Himmler's family as an exchange for Andrée de Jongh with MI6 and others. We believe the offering of such a pardon would only point out to the SS that de Jongh is a very valuable asset to us and therefore put her in more danger than she already is. Your request has been denied.

Also, in case you are disappointed, Ike said, "NO FUCKING WAY!"

Langley.

Cresswell wadded the paper up and threw it against the wall.

Chapter 28

❧

RAVENSBRÜCK PRISON
DECEMBER 1944

The evening appell had swelled to well over thirty thousand prisoners as Dedee rushed from the revier to the appellplatz. She was worried about Pauline, whom she had had to help to get to the morning count. The risk of punishment for assisting another prisoner had virtually disappeared because the number of prisoners was so high. She took her place in a row of five of the prisoners in her block, but she didn't see Pauline.

Grim made her count for the block. She knew Pauline was sick, which put her in a dilemma. She could lie and report a full count, and if she was caught, she would lose her job and probably go to the bunker, or she could report the count as one short, at which time the guards with their dogs would go into the block and find Pauline wherever she was hiding. From a distance, the faint drone of Allied bombers could be heard, probably returning to England. Grim did a quick recount, scribbled her number on the docket sheet and handed it to the guard.

Dedee allowed herself a sigh of relief when they were dismissed. Grim had lied. Maybe it was the sound of the bombers that was softening the blockova.

Dedee rushed back to her block.

She found Pauline lying on the floor near the toilets in her own blood and excrement. She was too weak to get up. Dedee used a wet rag to wipe the filth off her friend as best she could, then, with the help of another prisoner, carried Pauline back to their bunk. Dedee was skin and bones herself, and she knew it, but Pauline, who had been about Dedee's height and size when they'd first arrived, was much lighter. Dedee thought she could fly away in a stiff wind.

The next day was Sunday, and that evening, nearly three hundred women listened intently to Dedee as she reviewed some of the war-related items she had read during the week. They now had a radio in the hospital.

Pauline had had a better day, and she lay on their bunk with her head propped up, seemingly anxious to hear the news. "The Red Army has completely liberated Romania," Dedee said. The women broke out in raucous cheers, and Dedee had to wait before the dozen or so Romanians in particular quieted down. She particularly enjoyed delivering the news, she even adopted a newsreel staccato delivery.

"With major assistance from the Canadian Army, Belgium is totally liberated." The women were giddy and applauded loudly. Dedee wondered if she would ever see Brussels again.

"Axis forces ceded mainland Greece."

"Patton's Third Army crosses the Moselle and attacks the Germans holding Metz."

"Antwerp becomes the most important port for the Allies bringing war material into Europe."

Dedee thought if the block had any extra room, the women would have danced for joy. She was amazed at the hidden energy they had found.

Their excitement rekindled Dedee's. With an end to the war drawing near, she knew future events could be totally unpredictable. How the SS would take defeat was difficult to guess.

Pauline was worse the next morning, and again Grim covered for her.

When Dedee entered the revier after appell, she was told to see Triete first thing. That morning, his task of certifying the deaths of prisoners who were shot had been easy, because very few prisoners were selected to be killed on Sundays. They both arrived at his office at the same time, and he asked her in and closed the door.

"I'm afraid I have some very bad news," he said in a quiet voice. "A high official from Berlin is coming here tomorrow. His name is Lischka, a colonel in the SS who used to be the head of the Gestapo in Paris, I believe." Triete leveled his eyes at Dedee. "He's looking for somebody they say guided hundreds of downed Allied pilots back to England."

Dedee slumped in her chair.

"He's looking for Andrée de Jongh."

Dedee stood and took a deep breath. It was the one thing that had kept her from rejoicing when the good war news came. They must have finally figured it out. She thanked the doctor and left to perform her daily duties. When she returned to her block for soup, she whispered her situation to Pauline. Pauline squeezed Dedee's hand before she returned to the revier.

The afternoon dragged by slowly as Dedee fought to come up with a plan. She was sure that if Lischka could identify her, she would be shot. She saw no reason why they would delay her execution. She wished Langerfeld was still at the prison. She might have been able to help. Dedee thought about Triete. Would he help her? She worked her way to his office, but he had already left for the day. She wondered if he might have anticipated her request for help and left to avoid being asked to help. She thought about hiding. She had heard that some of the prisoners in other blocks were hiding some of the Rabbits. Maybe that was the best way. Possibly she could hide in the space between the ceiling and the roof in her barrack. But if she did, and was found anyway, she would be endangering the rest of the block.

Dedee had always relied on her wits and her ability to out-think her adversaries, but for the first time in her life, she had no idea what to do. She remembered telling new recruits to her line that the chances were very good they would captured or killed. She came to the slow realization that she would face whatever came and take it with her chin up, knowing she had made a difference.

During the evening appell, the droning of returning Allied bombers filled the air, as wave upon wave of planes headed back to England. Again, she wondered if Jack was up there, and the thought that one of them might be him, and that she was partially responsible for him being there, lifted her spirits as she marched back to her block.

She saw Pauline resting peacefully in their bunk. A sheet had been pulled up over her face and when Dedee pulled the sheet down, she saw that Pauline had wrapped a thin piece of cloth around her neck and tied it tight. Her face was purple and her body was cool. She quickly removed the cloth strip and noticed a note in Pauline's hand. She gently shook her friend's thin shoulder and whispered her name. No response. When Dedee checked her pulse, she confirmed what she had expected. Pauline was dead.

Dedee had known Pauline's death was inevitable, but she wasn't ready for it to turn out this way. Tears flowing freely down her cheeks, she picked up the note and as she did, a needle and thread fell from Paulin's other hand.

The note was barely legible.

You are Pauline Longet and your number is 120877. I am Andrée de Jongh, number 120841. Goodbye, dear friend.

She glanced over at Pauline's red triangle. Sewn onto the bottom was: 120841. Dedee let out a low, mournful wail, and wept.

Chapter 29

⧉

JANUARY 1945

The gold nordic cross on the Swedish flag affixed to the vertical stabilizer shone bright in the winter morning sun when the Junkers Ju 52 Tri-motor touched down at Berlin-Templehof Airport just south of the center of Berlin. The plane had to avoid bomb craters and damaged aircraft as it taxied to a stop near a large hangar. A tall, aristocratic man stepped down from the plane and got into the backseat of a waiting Mercedes sedan with Nazi flags mounted on the two front fenders.

The man in the backseat was Count Folke Bernadotte, who had been chosen by the Swedish government to negotiate with Heinrich Himmler the release of Swedish prisoners held in German camps. The car was driven to the Swedish Embassy, where Bernadotte conferred with the ambassador, Arvid Richert, about the meeting with Himmler. Richert informed Bernadotte that despite what Himmler's aides may have said, Hitler's stern orders were that no prisoners in any of the concentration camps should be alive when and if the camp was taken by Russian or Allied forces. As this order from Hitler was sharply different from Himmler's hint to the West, Bernadotte knew he had to be careful. The negotiations would be delicate.

They waited several days before Himmler finally said he would meet them. The venue was to be a clinic operated by Himmler's close friend, Doctor Karl Gebhardt, north of Berlin near Ravensbrück. Gebhardt was the chief surgeon on the staff of the SS Reich Physicians, and was Himmler's personal physician. More notably, he was the coordinator of all the surgical experiments at Ravensbrück and Auschwitz. Gebhardt told Bernadotte that his clinic was filled with children being treated for broken and lost limbs caused by Allied bombing.

The Reichfüher of the SS, Heinrich Himmler, entered the room. Wearing an unadorned green Waffen-SS uniform, the short, bespectacled man looked nothing like his reputation. The only hints of his rank were his countenance, his manicured nails, and his air of intellectual superiority. He shook the taller Bernadotte's hand and seemed impressed with his nobility, bowing ever so slightly.

Bernadotte listened patiently as Himmler ranted about how, even though the odds were slim, the Reich could ultimately survive. Eventually, Bernadotte found the opportunity to propose the plan to free his fellow Swedes, to which Himmler initially reacted angrily, repeating over and over again the Führer's orders to exterminate them, and his extreme loyalty to the Führer himself. Bernadotte let him vent, and eventually his tone softened. After three hours, Himmler had agreed to let a Swedish task force pick up various Scandinavian prisoners and take them to Sweden.

The agreement was more than Bernadotte had hoped, but more importantly, he was convinced Himmler was scared. Bernadotte knew he would be seeing the Reichfüher again soon.

Chapter 30

rim was in trouble. For the past several days, her count at appell had been one short because Pauline was hiding. Now, at the early morning count, her count had to include the dead Pauline. One of the SS guards had figured out that Grim had included the then bedridden Pauline in her previous counts. She was exposed as being in collusion with the other inmates, and she was sent to the detention bunker.

Dedee, who had sewn Pauline's number onto her own red triangle, felt sorry for Grim. She knew Grim would be beaten, and her chances of survival were not good. Just after Pauline's death, Dedee had informed Grim that she had taken Pauline's identity. Grim, who had heard of others in different blocks doing the same thing, had simply nodded and walked away. Dedee thought the timing of the day's events would be critical.

For the first time in weeks, Dedee spent the night without hearing Pauline's terrible, deep coughing. Pauline lay next to her making no sound, as her body grew colder and colder. Not being able to sleep and feeling guilt for Pauline's sacrifice, Dedee put her arms around her dead friend, and tried to make sense of it all.

With Grim gone and a replacement blockova not yet chosen, one of the guards took Grim's place at the head of Dedee's
block. The count took much longer than usual, and even though
Dedee's view was blocked, she figured out that the delay was
caused by the arrival of the SS colonel Triete had warned her
of. Whenever a dignitary of higher rank visited the prison, the
guards took their jobs much more seriously.

Finally, the counts were accepted by the new head guard,
who announced that all the blocks were to report to their work
duties, with the exception of Dedee's block. After all the other blocks were gone, Dedee's was ordered to form two parallel
lines across the lagerplatz. The tone of the orders changed from
routine to demanding. When the two lines were formed, Major
Suhren, the prison superintendent, appeared, accompanied by
an SS colonel. The colonel was tall, erect, and wore spectacles.
He held two pictures in his hand, and the two men slowly walked
down the row, comparing each prisoner's face with them. Dedee
realized he was probably the man in charge of investigations into
French Resistance organizations, and if so, he was responsible
for the deaths of countless French and Belgian patriots. This was
the infamous Kurt Lischka. In addition, if they were looking for
her, then either her father had broken and confessed or someone
else in the organization had been tortured into identifying her.

Whatever the case, she was nearly positive Paul was dead.
She hoped otherwise, but her practical side said he was gone.
Just before they reached the end of the front line, they ordered
a prisoner to step forward. Dedee could hear the creak of their
leather boots as they moved to the second line and worked their
way closer to her. With her eyes straight forward, Dedee felt like
she was waiting for the blade of a guillotine to drop. Every muscle in her body was tense. She felt her eyelids quivering.

She remembered her old trick of trying to relax. She started
with her feet and moved up to her calves, concentrating on each
area, forcing the tension out. As she moved up, she could feel
herself breathing easier.

Then the two officers were directly in front of her. She could smell their breath. Suhren held the picture up beside Dedee's ear and the two of them compared the image to the woman. Dedee kept her eyes straight ahead, looking through the two officers, not at them. Suhren shook his head, but Lischka took her by the arm and pulled her forward one step. They moved on down the line.

When they had finished the second line, Suhren dismissed everyone but Dedee and the prisoner they had selected from the front row. Dedee started with her feet again.

They went to the first woman and, although Dedee couldn't hear them clearly appeared to ask her questions. They kept their voices low, but Dedee could see they were showing more photographs to the woman. Dedee visualized what kind of pictures they might be showing to the other woman. They could only be pictures of either her friends or her father. Dedee braced herself and started to build her wall of snow.

Then the two men approached her. Standing eye-to-eye with her, Lischka spoke in a matter-of-fact tone. "Your father, I believe you call him Paul, told us everything. Of course, he refused at first, but when we pulled out his fingernails he loosened up."

Dedee managed to contain the surge of emotion those words elicited.

"But he really told us the whole story when we stuck a knife up his rectum." Lischka's eyes studied Dedee's, watching for a reaction. Even a sudden dilation of her pupils would give her away.

Dedee held on, but she felt her snow wall melting. She concentrated on keeping her breath slow and steady.

Suhren held a picture in front of her. Dedee didn't want to look, but when he shook it, demanding her attention, she let her eyes turn slowly to the image. It was Paul, lying on the ground, face up, covered in blood. He had been shot though the neck from behind.

Dedee forced herself to smile.

"You think this is funny?" Suhren asked.

"My father died at Verdun during the Great War," she said lightly.

Dumbfounded, the two men walked away. Lischka said, "sie its sowieso zu klein." *She's too little anyway.*

Chapter 31

❧

B y the time that evening's appell was over, nearly everyone in the block knew that Dedee de Jongh, aka Pauline Longet, had survived and outsmarted the Gestapo. When she entered, she was embarrassed by the cheering from that group of women who had so little to cheer about. Dedee's first concern was Grim, and she vowed to find a way to get her out of the strafsblock. A new blockova had not yet been chosen, so after the lights were turned out, the women were left unattended.

During the next weeks, the influx of prisoners further strained the ability of the staff to maintain any kind of control. Food supplies became even scarcer. Toilet facilities were strained beyond capacity and ditches were dug along the outside walls of the barracks, nearest the prison walls. Despite the winter weather, the latrines became infested with flies and reeked of sewage.

A gas chamber had been constructed on the outside wall next to the ovens, which spewed greasy black smoke twenty-four hours a day. The total number of prisoners exceeded forty thousand in a camp designed to handle ten thousand. When the gas chamber could not keep up with the killing, they used two buses. The buses were sealed, and when loaded to capacity, an open

can of poisonous gas was thrown in through a small hole near
the engine. Ten minutes later, the bodies would be unloaded into
the crematorium. Still, the continued influx of new prisoners far
exceeded the number exterminated.

Since she had assumed Pauline's identity, Dedee also assumed her work detail. Her job each day was to gather pieces of
wood that others had split and stack them onto wheelbarrows,
which were then wheeled to the crematorium to be used to fuel
the ovens. During her time at the camp, Dedee's muscles had
atrophied. Even small pieces of wood required an effort to pick
up, pieces that several years ago she would have tossed with one
hand. Her legs, which had always been stronger than average,
now looked like the knobby outer limbs of a tree. She thought
again of Jack. He would have had to carry *her* over the Pyrenees.

She realized that she was starving to death, and that it was
being hastened by the energy she expended on her work detail.
The empty pain in her stomach had been with her for so long, she
wondered what it would feel like if she could eat a real meal. She
had long ago ceased to menstruate, her breasts had shrunk, she
was severely constipated, and her pulse rate was much higher
than normal. She had to find a way to survive, to see Jack again.
She thought about the nights they had slept next to each other
and the sheer pleasure simply of his presence beside her. Would
it ever happen again? Sometimes, when she lay on her bunk,
exhausted, trying to sleep, she remembered when they met. But
her mind was so foggy, she questioned whether Jack had ever
really existed, and wasn't some kind of prop her confused mind
had conjured up.

Chapter 32

∾⧉∾

MARCH 1945

W e're just crossing the German border," the captain announced. "We'll land in less than an hour." The Junkers aircraft had to fly just above the treetops. The flight was secret, and they needed to avoid all other aircraft. In the backseat was Count Bernadotte on his way to a second important meeting with Himmler. Since their first meeting, when Himmler had given permission to rescue some Scandinavians, the Swedes had been successful. With dozens of buses, ambulances, and trucks accompanied by hundreds of nurses and doctors, over five thousand prisoners had been rescued from Sachsenhausen, Dachau, and other nearby concentration camps. These Scandinavian prisoners were taken to a well-prepared Swedish holding center near Friedrichsruh on the northern border of Germany. Bernadotte's buses had not been able to go to the women at Ravensbrück, however, as Bernadotte had not been given permission to go there.

This time, Bernadotte wanted that permission. Specifically, he was seeking permission to evacuate the French prisoners. Bernadotte was of French blood. A direct descendant of Jean-Baptist Bernadotte, one of Napoleon's marshals. Also, during the rescues at Dauchau, while they were only permitted to rescue Scandinavians, other nationalities had also been rescued, as the bus drivers couldn't refuse the other desperate prisoners, begging for help. Bernadotte was banking on the same at Ravensbrück.

Again, they landed at Berlin-Templehof, but this time they were driven to Hohenlychen, a sanitarium in northern Berlin. On the way, the driver had to take many detours around bomb craters and the rubble of destroyed buildings. As Bernadotte saw the scope of Berlin's devastation, his mission became far more urgent. As far as he knew, the order from Hitler to eradicate all prisoners before the Russians or the Allies came still stood. From the news he had received, the Russians were just weeks or even days away from Ravensbrück.

Himmler's demeanor was much different this time. He was fidgety and irritable. Walter Schellenberg and his adjutant were seated in a huge parlor with Himmler pacing in front of them. He spoke for nearly twenty minutes of his loyalty to Hitler and his absolute German duty to obey the Führer's orders. Bernadotte saw little opportunity to press his wishes, and finally Himmler excused himself to make a phone call. When Bernadotte and Schellenberg were alone, Schellenberg said Himmler had authorized him to ask Bernadotte to act as an intermediary and go directly to Eisenhower to allow Himmler to negotiate an armistice with the western Allies. Bernadotte, leaving no doubt on the table, quickly told Schellenberg that he could not do such a thing, whereupon, Schellenberg left the room to tell Himmler. They returned shortly and surprisingly, Himmler did not seem upset.

Addressing Himmler, Bernadotte asked, "I would like your permission, sir, to rescue all the Scandinavians held throughout Germany and take them back to Sweden."

"Not possible," Himmler said. "That would be a direct disobedience of Hitler's standing order. Taking large numbers like that would certainly draw his attention, and I cannot do that." His voice was matter of fact and without emotion.

"How about just the release of the Norwegian and Swedish women?" Bernadotte shrewdly countered.

Himmler took off his glasses, held them to the light, and wiped them with his handkerchief. "Yes," he said. "That would be possible," then he signaled the meeting was over.

While Bernadotte had not specifically included the French, he knew his bus drivers would not leave them behind, and his buses were now allowed to go into Ravensbrück. As his plane took off and headed north, Bernadotte took out a small brandy flask from is pocket and offered a toast to no one. "Here's to you, Riechfüher Himmler, you rotten son-of-a-bitch."

Chapter 33

❧

At appell the next morning, the count was taken quickly, with little or no attention at accuracy. The SS prison staff were in confusion. Suhren's orders were the cause. As camp commandant, he answered directly to Himmler; however, Hitler's orders were different. Himmler hoped to gain a back-channel peace negotiation and possibly save his own life, versus Hitler, who had no such aspirations and wanted all prisoners dead. Suhren's staff were also divided between those who wanted the prisoners to speak kindly of them when the Russians came and the ones who wanted no witnesses at all. The gassings and cremations continued and the sweet, putrid smell hung in the still air, nauseating the prisoners. An odor that survivors would never forget.

Dedee now worked in a forested area nearly a mile from the prison. For some unknown reason, their morning coffee had had some real coffee in it, and everyone in her block had received an extra piece of bread. This did not assuage her hunger, but she had a bit more energy. Each morning she hoped to see Grim, but the blockova was still being held in the bunker.

Dedee had hoped Triete would intervene. Triete was also looking out for his own survival, and he had expressed his desire to help.

Around mid-morning, the sun broke through the clouds, and uplifted the workers' spirits. The guards were relaxed, and Dedee moved slowly, picking up one small piece of wood at a time and loading it into a wheelbarrow.

She heard the soft drone of approaching vehicles, and looking out through the trees, she saw white buses with red crosses painted on the sides. Dozens of them drove past, heading for the prison front gate. The significance of the white buses took a moment to sink in, however, but when the buses parked immediately in front of the gates, the work crew threw up their arms and cheered.

A polish woman working next to Dedee grabbed her and yelled, "Wolnosc jestesmy uwalniani" *Freedom, we are being freed!* over and over in jubilation.

Dedee joined the celebration, hugging her workmates.

Soon, the whole work crew was dancing in a circle with their arms around each other. The guards stood by stoically, not knowing what to make of the buses. The prisoners talked excitedly to each other in several different languages, and incredibly, they all understood exactly what the other was saying. At the end of the work shift, they went back to the prison, and they passed the buses on the way through the front gate. Dedee could see inside them, and noted many were equipped with cots, stacked on the sides. Each bus had a uniformed driver and two nurses. The drivers' uniforms had the white-on-red Swiss Cross on the arms, while the buses bore the red-on-white Red Cross flag.

Inside the gates, rumors were rampant; however, the prevailing opinion was that these Swiss buses had only come for French women, and they only had enough room for about three hundred. Dedee immediately thought of Pauline, and how, if she were still alive, she might have been liberated. Then she thought of herself. Even though she was Belgian, she *had* assumed a French identity. Would Pauline be on the list of French women slated to go? She knew she was starving, but she could just look around and see hundreds, even thousands of women in much worse physical condition. More than anything, she wanted to be on one of those buses, but if she was, how could she live with herself?

After evening appell, Dedee walked back to her barrack, and there on her bunk lay Grim. She was barely recognizable. He hair was matted with blood and her arms were covered with welts and bruises. She turned her head toward Dedee as she approached. Her eyes were both badly bruised, and one was nearly swollen shut. Her forehead was covered with sweat.

"Care to share your bunk? I'm no longer your blockova," she said weakly.

"My God, Grim, what have they done to you?"

"I told them nothing."

"And therefore, I'm still alive." Dedee put her hand on Grim's arm and said she would be right back.

She returned with a wet rag and wiped some of the blood from Grim's face. The wounds were old and had scabbed over. Dedee was shocked at how much weight her former blockova she had lost. Her arms were twig-like, and the skin hung down loosely. Grim closed her eyes and fell into a deep sleep.

Dedee tended to her sleeping friend. Her pulse was weak and fast, and Dedee realized Grim was very sick. When she tried to wake her to share some soup that evening, Grim would not awaken.

Even though the buses may only have come French prisoners, many thought there would be others. Some thought that the next buses might come for Poles, then Russians, taking them home by nationality. This made sense. Why would a bus want to take Russians west? The one thing the members of Dedee's block had that they had not had the night before was hope.

After appell the next morning, Dedee found Grim awake and got her to eat some soup. Grim was having chills, and Dedee realized she needed medication to fight whatever kind of infection she had. Dedee got her down from the bunk and helped her walk to the revier. A German nurse took one look at Grim and immediately put her in a bed while Dedee explained her symptoms. The nurse was German, and Dedee asked if Doctor Triete was on duty. The nurse said he was and left.

A short time later, Triete entered the room. "You, again?" he said. "I see you have a new patient. Not tuberculosis this time?"

He went over to Grim and, after checking her pulse, ran his hands over her lower abdomen. He noted Grim's cuts and bruises, and examined each one. "They're calling for all the French prisoners to line up outside. Shouldn't you be out there?"

"I'm not French," Dedee said.

"Longet. Longet is not French?"

"Truthfully, doctor, I don't know what I am. I just want to be sure this woman gets better."

"I think she has some internal injuries. She has had a rough time of it." His voice lowered. "You know she will not be safe here. They will want to get rid of her. Our days here are almost over and they want to destroy all evidence that prisoners were mistreated. Just this morning, two of my patients who were in a similar condition were shot. I've given up asking questions, but I know how much is two and two."

"Give me the medicine. I will take care of her."

"You could probably get out of here on one of those buses. Be on your way home." He said it almost like a question.

"This woman almost died for me. The least I can do is try to get her well. There are a lot of kind people still left in this world," she said. "Two of them are in this room, and I'm not one of them."

Triete went to a medicine cabinet and gave Dedee a packet of pills. "This will take care of her infection." he said. "And, you *are* one of them. The kind ones, I mean."

With the help of a nurse, Dedee brought Grim back to her block.

A prisoner whose bunk was near Dedee's told her the name 'Pauline Longet' had been called, and if she hurried, she could still make it. Dedee tilted Grim's head forward to give her a pill.

"I will leave when Grim does," Dedee said, wiping Grim's brow.

After three days of frustrating delay, 299 French prisoners boarded the Swiss buses and departed for the nearly 500-mile journey to the Swiss border and freedom.

⸎

Three days after the French had departed, another convoy of white buses approached the front gates. This time they were looking for Scandinavians. While Dedee was happy more buses had arrived, she was concerned about Grim. The former blocko-va had been slow to respond to the medication. Dedee spent as much time as she could tending to her friend and making sure she was comfortable.

One restless night, Grim gave a start when she saw Dedee lying beside her in their bunk. "You're still here," Grim whispered.

Dedee stroked Grim's forehead, brushing her hair out of her eyes. "Of course I am. Please try to go back to sleep."

Grim was quiet for a while, then said. "Why are you helping me? You should have left with the French. You don't even know me."

"You saved my life. You could have told the SS I was the person they were looking for, and you didn't. I don't know why you did that, but I won't leave you here."

"But I slapped you."

Dedee pulled the blanket up, making sure Grim was warm. "Try to go back to sleep," she said. She rolled over and wondered if she would ever get out of Ravensbrück.

Chapter 34

APRIL 1945

Count Bernadotte prepared for one more meeting with Himmler. With the white buses having departed Ravensbrück, he knew that he had very little time to get more of the women out before the Russians arrived. The pervasive feeling among the Swedish delegation was the SS would conduct a mass slaughter before the Russians came through, and there was a sense of extreme urgency for another meeting. Himmler's staff, principally Walter Schellenberg and his assistant Franz Göring, had kept channels of communication open during the last few days, with hopes that eventually the West would see in Himmler a conduit for peace negotiations.

Taking a plane into the bowels of war-torn Germany was not possible, so Bernadotte had taken a night train to Malmo, then a ferry to Copenhagen. From there a staff car drove him into Germany, and during a lull in the bombing, he arrived at the Swedish legation in Berlin. The bombing started again, so Bernadotte took shelter in the basement, during which he was able to make contact with Schellenberg, who reported he did not know where Himmler was. Bernadotte was later to learn that Himmler was actually in a bunker with Hitler, celebrating Hitler's birthday.

After several hours, Schellenberg notified Bernadotte that Himmler would meet him at Hohenlychen, the same place as before. They drove north again, passing Rheinsberg, very close to Ravensbrück. The darkened horizon was lit up to the east with Russian artillery fire and Katyusha rocket detonations. Bernadotte thought he might be too late. When they arrived at Hohenlychen, he was met by Karl Gebhardt again, who graciously welcomed him and told him Himmler had been detained. They had dinner, and Himmler still had not arrived once they had finished.

In the early hours of the next day, Himmler arrived and when he greeted Bernadotte with "Guten tag," instead of the requisite, 'Heil Hitler,' he knew the situation was changing rapidly. Himmler, dressed in a perfectly pressed uniform adorned with medals, immediately reviewed the Reich's history, although he said nothing about its now inevitable defeat.

Himmler appeared tired. He kept tapping his front teeth together, a trait Schellenberg had said was a sign he was weary. The discussion turned immediately to the release of Ravensbrück prisoners, and Bernadotte asked for the immediate release of all the remaining French women.

Himmler nodded, then added. "Sie konnen all nationalitaten nehmen." *You can take all nationalities.* Then he threw up his hands as if his business was concluded, and left.

Goring left the room with Bernadotte and in the hall, they both agreed Göring should go straight to Ravensbrück to personally deliver Himmler's instructions.

Chapter 35

RAVENSBRÜCK PRISON

THE NEXT DAY

"You give me orders from Himmler to release these prisoners," Suhren told Franz Göring. "And, I have orders from the Führer himself that I must liquidate each and every one before the Russians get here. What am I to do?"

"The Führer may already be dead," Göring replied.

Suhren stared at his once-shiny black boots. After several moments, he said, "I have fifteen thousand Westerners. Take them. Take them straight away."

The news that all the Western prisoners were to be freed spread through the camp. Dedee was sitting next to Grim when she heard. Grim was sleeping, and Dedee shook her arm to wake her.

"We're to be freed," Dedee said when Grim awoke.

Grim, who had the previous day walked a short distance for the first time since returning to the barrack, replied that she could not believe it. Dedee's block was almost entirely from the West, and pandemonium ensued as they all streamed outside into the lagerplatz to celebrate. Dedee kept Grim quiet. She wanted her to save her energy. She was sure Grim would need it if and when they ever got outside the prison walls.

Grim asked, "What's the first thing you will do when you get home?"

"I know my father is dead, but I hope my mother is alive, and if she is, I'm going to ask her to make a big casserole of carbonnade a la flamande, and then I will sit down and eat it all by myself." Dedee giggled, and wondered when the last time she had had a real laugh had been.

"You know, Grim," she said. "I do not know your first name. You're the only friend I have here in this godforsaken place, and I don't even know you."

"Theresa," she said. "After my grandmother."

"Lovely." Dedee hesitated. "Why didn't you tell them who I really was before they beat you? What made you do it? You could have told them, and you would have avoided all this."

"When they were beating me, I asked myself that same question so many times. I think it was because I didn't like myself. I didn't like what I had become. I mean I didn't really want to be a blockova, but when I saw the better food and more privileges, I gave it a try. But these SS are smart. Eventually I found out I was trapped. They are masters at using people. I had to be cruel and I'm not that way. It was like being in a narrow alley with a car coming at you from the front and another from the rear. So, when you said those nice words to me about being a good blockova, I saw that even under the worst of conditions people can be kind. That's when I decided I had had enough, and I took a stand."

"I admire you for that," Dedee said.

Gradually, the prisoners came back to their respective blocks.

While the women in the Russian and other Eastern blocks had nothing to cheer about, Western European women who had been hiding from certain death started to come out of their long-held hiding places. They appeared from holes in the ceilings and from false walls in the shower rooms. Two Dutch women who had been on one of Suhren's death lists emerged from a hole they had dug behind a toilette. They were covered in filth, but they were alive, having been fed for weeks by other prisoners in their block. They were told to be ready to leave at five o'clock the next morning.

With their meager belongings in small bags or just stuffed into their pockets, the prisoners who expected to be freed started to assemble in the lagerplatz before the five o'clock siren. The temperature had dropped in the night, and a cold rain immediately soaked the prisoners' thin clothing. They stood at attention, in rows of five. Dedee had helped Theresa to the lagerplatz and they stood side-by-side waiting for the head guard to tell them what to do.

No one came.

Dawn approached, and the rain came down harder. Dedee saw that Theresa was shivering. The ground was saturated, and Dedee could see the water around Theresa's feet shaking as she trembled. Two hours later, the head guard, with an umbrella, came to the front of the lines and announced that there had been a delay. Two buses came near the front gate and parked so everyone could see them. They weren't white, and Dedee knew them immediately for what they were, the makeshift gas chambers. The brick-and-mortar gas chambers had been torn down several days prior, in anticipation of the Russian arrival, but the buses were still in use. The prisoners, who had been expecting to be freed, were now stricken with fear.

The guards went inside, out of the rain.

After another hour, some of the women fell to the ground. Silently, with their hopes shattered, they collapsed, yielding to their misery. Dedee, feeling the last bits of energy escape her, saw Theresa's legs start to falter, and she moved over and put her arm around her waist and held her up.

Another hour passed.

Dedee felt like her mind and body had been cleaved. She built her wall and hid behind it, isolating herself from the cold, the rain, and despair. She thought about what Hell might be like, and realized she was already there. Women dropped all around her.

The head guard finally came out around noon. The front gates opened and they were told to march forward, and that if anyone was unable, they would be left behind. The lines of five broke down. The prisoners who could walk didn't trust the guards. They thought they were going to be gassed. Dedee, with her arm still supporting Theresa, pushed forward one step at a time. They passed through the front gates, and reached the two gassing buses. Dedee held her breath as a guard stopped them and ripped their triangles off their clothing. They struggled forward and for the first time, they realized they were not just another number. Theresa found some modicum of energy, knowing that this was it. Freedom was within reach.

In the distance, near the woods where Dedee had gathered wood, were dozens of white buses, all emblazoned with red crosses. Dedee saw men standing in front of them, dressed in blue uniforms with yellow, Swedish crosses on their chests and caps. Many were blond, and most were smiling, approaching the women to help them to the buses.

As these men saw the condition of the women, some cried. These were the first men Dedee had seen in a long time with kindness written on their faces. With a tall Swede helping Theresa, they boarded the first bus, and were met by a nurse, who assisted them to a seat and gave them each a box with a red cross on it. Each box contained pieces of fruit, sandwiches, a jar of water and a damp cloth.

When the buses were ready to pull out, Dedee's was the first in line. The driver spoke in French and told them that the convoy would split up due air attacks. They were to take the Schrwerin

Road to Demark through Lubeck, while the others would take a more northerly route. The Germans were painting red crosses on the top of their retreating trucks, and the Allied fighter planes were having difficulty determining the Red Cross buses from the German fakes. He told them that the trip would be long and they might have delays.

When the buses started to roll, the women cheered. Several of them lay on the stacked cots but their jubilance was clear. One French prisoner in the front started to sing. Softly at first, then as others joined in, their voices grew firm and strong as they sang *La Marseillaise*.

> Allons enfants de la Patrie,
> Le jour de gloire est arrivé!
> Contre nous de la tyrannie,
> L'étendard sanglant est levé,
> Entendez-vous dans les campagnes
> Mugir ces féroces soldats?
> Ils viennent jusque dans vos bras
> Égorger vos fils, vos compagnes!

> *Rise children of the fatherland*
> *The day of glory has arrived*
> *Against us tyranny's*
> *Bloody standard is raised*
> *Listen to the sound in the fields*
> *The howling of these fearsome soldiers*
> *They are coming into our midst*
> *To cut the throats of your sons and consorts!*

When they got to the chorus, everyone who could stood.

> Aux armes, citoyens,
> Formez vos bataillons,
> Marchons, marchons!

Qu'un sang impur
Abreuve nos sillons!

To arms citizens
Form your battalions
March! March!
Let impure blood
Water our furrows!

Dedee and nearly everyone in the bus, including the driver, had tears of joy streaming down their faces. Many did not understand the words of, but few doubted the song expressed their emotions.

The road was full of swelling crowds of refugees and columns of retreating German soldiers. The soldiers looked dejected, their heads down and their shoulders slumped. The driver maneuvered cautiously around bomb craters, abandoned cars, the debris of war. At one point, they passed an overturned white bus that had been headed the other way.

Some in the bus had drunk water given to them when they'd boarded the bus several hours before, and they asked the driver to stop so they could relieve themselves. He pulled over near a grassy pasture. Dedee and most of the others got out and crossed over a ditch into the field, which was covered with fresh spring grass and dotted with dandelions. When the women saw the yellow flowers, they forgot about the need to relieve themselves and gorged themselves on the blossoms. Then they took sticks and dug up the rhizomes, shook the dirt off, and ate them whole, all the while savoring a taste many had almost forgotten. Dedee picked a few extra for Theresa, who eagerly attacked them, smacking her lips.

They hadn't gone another half mile when the bus stopped abruptly and the driver said they were being attacked. He told them to get off the bus, as he had seen a fighter plane approaching just ahead. His voice was urgent and the women piled out and lay down in the ditch beside the road. The plane came roaring toward them no more than a hundred feet in the air. Dedee heard the scream of the plane's engine, and covered Theresa as best she could. The plane, a British Spitfire, flew directly over them, and as he passed, he pulled back on the stick and climbed, gently rocking his wings. Dedee remembered Jack telling her he wanted to be a fighter pilot. She imagined him in the Spitfire, rocking his wings. That would be something he would do.

Dedee had the sense that they were nearing the battle line that separated the two armies. The bus pulled over several times to let light tanks go by. The tanks were covered with tree limbs for camouflage and the driver's heads stuck up above the armor without helmets. Many had desperate, bloodshot eyes. Troop carriers sped past towing howitzers that fishtailed behind them as the drivers rushed toward Berlin. The bus driver pulled over again and stopped. Through his windshield, Dedee could see a small village ahead. Several buildings were in flames, and black smoke rose into the air. She saw a German soldier running toward the bus several hundred feet ahead, and he suddenly stopped, stood up straight, and fell to the ground. The bus driver ordered everyone out of the bus and into the drainage ditch alongside the road as another white bus pulled up behind them.

The women quickly got out and scattered up and down the ditch, which flowed with water from the recent rains. Dedee had to help Theresa, and they lay down together in the ditch with Dedee partially covering Theresa for protection. The cold water soaked through Dedee's already damp clothing to her skin, chilling her.

She heard the scream of the Spitfire before she saw it. It appeared over the village and came directly at them with his eight wing-mounted cannons belching fire. Dedee pulled Theresa closer. She could hear the bullets hit the water all around them.

She felt a splash of mud hit her cheek and the whole side of her face went numb. And then the plane was gone. The driver waited several minutes before he yelled an all clear to get back in the bus.

Dedee put her hand to her cheek, and as she did, she saw blood dripping from her arm. She saw fresh blood in the water streaming past. She looked to Theresa.

Theresa had a hole in her abdomen and another in her chest. She was dead. The bullet that had grazed Dedee's arm had hit Theresa in the chest. Her eyes were still open. She looked bewildered.

Dedee didn't say a word. She crawled up and sat on the side of the ditch and stared at her friend, who had finally found her way. She thought how she must have suffered in the bunker, hanging onto her belief that she could be a better person. Dedee did not cry, she was beyond that.

Chapter 36

❧

A red sun was setting in the west when Dedee's bus finally pulled in to the Red Cross camp just across the border. Nurses and doctors greeted them, waving and smiling. They were taken into a large area where they were given porridge and hot milk. They had been cautioned to eat slowly, so Dedee took her time and swallowed her food deliberately, knowing that if she ate it too fast, it would come back up. She especially savored the warm milk. She almost felt like chewing it, it was so rich and full of fat. Those ex-prisoners who could walk were taken to rooms with beds covered in clean white sheets, and adjoining bathrooms and showers. A nurse told her she should sleep. She could shower in the morning. Dedee took off her clothes and fell into bed, utterly exhausted. She looked up at the ceiling and the soft glow of the fluorescent lights. She heard the gentle hum of the generators, and her heavy eyelids closed.

When she opened her eyes in the morning, she smelled the delicious aroma of real coffee, and she had to stop and remember where she was. She stood and looked at her bed and was embarrassed to see her sheets were covered with mud, blood, and grime from the ditch. The large room contained a row of beds against a windowed wall. Beside each bed was a nightstand with a lamp. Hanging on the end of each bed was a clipboard showing the patient's name. Dedee looked at her chart. It was blank. She walked to the bathroom and shower area, and saw her reflection in a mirror for the first time in two years. She looked behind her. Her first thought had been that the reflection was someone else. She was horrified. Instead of seeing an attractive young woman, she was looking at a dirty, gray-haired, shriveled old hag. She had no breasts, and her arms were like twigs with her sallow skin hanging off them like droopy curtains. Her eyes were hollow, with black circles. Her cheekbones stuck out and the flesh around her mouth looked paper thin. She didn't know who the person in the mirror was. She only saw a cadaver. She turned away in shame.

She took a warm shower, relishing the soap suds. It had been years since she had used soap. She recalled Fresnes prison, when she'd had to clean the cell with only water. She had never thought of soap as a luxury before, but it is a luxury when there isn't any. Still uncomfortable seeing herself in the mirror, she combed her hair and tried to make herself look as good as possible, then she went back to her bed. The bed had been changed while she was showering. The nurse gave her a white, sheath dress, and a sweater, and told her she could have some breakfast and then she would then be evaluated by a doctor.

When the nurse was helping her with her new dress, Dedee leaned heavily against her.

"I feel faint," she said and fell into the nurse's arms.

Dedee awoke to the stinging smell of ammonia and the vision of a man in a white jacket passing a wad of cotton under her nose.

"You left us for quite a while," the man said. "I'm Doctor Hansen. How do you feel?" He spoke in German.

"I don't think I feel anything," Dedee responded in French. "Did I faint?"

"Yes, you did, and we let you rest for a couple of hours. Can you sit up?" His French was thick but understandable.

Doctor Hansen pulled a four-wheeled stool over to Dedee's bedside and prepared to write on the clipboard at its foot. "Please confirm your name."

"Dedee de Jongh."

"You are Belgian? When were you first captured?"

Dedee answered each question, and the doctor seemed satisfied, then he switched to another line. "Do you feel sad?"

"Sad?"

"Yes, you have gone through nearly two years of major trauma. These kinds of things affect people in different ways. Many suffer from anxiety and depression and I wonder about you."

"I'll need some time to answer that," Dedee said.

The doctor took her hand in his, turning her palm up. Running his finger over it, he asked, "Can you feel this?"

"I feel it on my palm but not on my fingers," she said.

The doctor did the same with her feet, and she reported only a tingling sensation in her toes. Then he asked her to lie down, and he examined her abdomen, noticing it was mildly distended. He checked her temperature and all of her vital signs. He asked her about her regularity, periods, and liquid intake.

After a thorough check, he took off his stethoscope and sat next to her on the bed.

"You're better than many of the others," he said. "You are a very sick lady, however, and you need a lot of care. We will put you on an IV to get you hydrated and on the road to healing. I want to keep you here for a couple of weeks, then you can go to Sweden, where they have better facilities, to promote a full recovery."

"When will I be able to go home?"

"When you are better. Please don't underestimate the severity of your condition. Another two or three weeks at Ravensbrück, and you would probably have been dead."

Dedee found the strength to smile. "Can I write home to my mother?" she asked.

AFTERWORD

❦

Dedee and her mother exited the cab and gawked at Buckingham Palace across the street from the Ruebens Hotel. Both marveled at its grandeur, the symbol of the monarchy that represented the British people as it had struggled to defeat Nazi Germany. Londoners were leaving their offices for the day, the horrors of the past six years seemingly forgotten.

When Dedee gave her name to the man behind the registration counter, he disappeared briefly and another man dressed in a coat and tie quickly took his place. "Miss de Jongh," he said. "We have been anxiously awaiting your arrival. Welcome to London and our hotel." He bowed to Dedee and her mother. "We have the Charles De Gaulle suite waiting for you, please follow me."

As they climbed the circular main stairway to the second floor, the man, who had explained he was the manager, told them that the De Gaulle suite had been the general's headquarters when he was in London just after the fall of Paris. The manager proudly told them that General de Gaulle came as a minor officer in the French Army and left as the leader of all the French people.

The suite consisted of a large, luxurious bedroom and sitting room. Dedee was taken aback by its opulence. The manager told them they were the guests of the grateful British people, and everything would be paid for. A bottle of Veuve Clicquot La Grande Dame sweated in an ice bucket on a desk in the corner. An enormous bouquet of red roses sat on the coffee table next to a bowl of fresh fruit. The richly wood paneled walls, high ceilings, and royal navy and gold decor gave the rooms a regal appearance.

When the manager left, Dedee's mother sat on the bed, sinking into the mattress. "What have you gotten us into?" she asked, smiling.

"They are showing their gratitude," Dedee said. She walked around the suite, admiring the paintings, vases, and furnishings. "I wish Paul was here to see this," she said.

With a sigh, her mother said, "I think he is."

Dedee had spent four weeks in the Danish hospital, then was transferred to Sweden, where she spent another four months recuperating from the ravages Ravensbrück had caused her body and mind. As word slowly got out that Andrée de Jongh, aka The Postwoman, had survived, she received mail from all over the world. She read and answered each one, and slowly came to terms with her guilt. She was plagued by the fact that she had been unable to save her father, and the image of him enduring torture continued to haunt her in her darkest hours. She also thought of the prisoners at Ravensbrück who had not yet left when she did, and how she could have stayed and helped them. Inevitably, she her thoughts returned to Jack. He occupied a special place in her mind, a safe area where she could go and find hope.

Some of the letters she received were from soldiers who had gone through the line and made it back to England. Many contained photographs: one from an American pilot from Texas, showed him sitting on a horse, holding a baby. Dedee would try to remind herself that she was in part responsible for that smile, or at least had helped make it possible. It helped.

Another was from a brash young Irish tail gunner whom Dedee remembered. His brogue was so thick no one could understand him. He was always talking, whether anyone understood him or not. Dedee recalled taking him through a checkpoint, and when the Vichy agent asked him a question, he said "aay," and the agent, recognizing he was probably a Brit, just motioned him through, shaking his head.

In a class by themselves were the marriage proposals. Some were jocular and tongue in cheek, but others were serious and written by smitten young men who did not know exactly how to express their gratitude. At least that was the way Dedee thought of it.

The letter from Jack, however, was on top of the pile. When he had learned of her survival and subsequent invitation from King George VI to come and receive the George Medal at Buckingham Palace, he had written, saying he looked forward to seeing her there. The letter had left her with contradicting emotions. On one hand, she wanted desperately to see him and be with him. On the other hand, she was afraid that he wouldn't be the same as the image she had of him.

One of the king's charges d'affaires came to their suite to tell Dedee of the plans for the next day. After private tours of the palace and grounds, a review for the divestiture ceremony was to be held shortly before the 5:00 PM start time. Dedee asked if it would be a private affair, to which the charges replied that many people would come just to see her. He said the RAF would be well represented, as would be MI6 and MI9. He didn't say anything about Jack, but even so, she felt a certain apprehension about appearing in front of the king and a crowd.

The next day, at fifteen minutes before five o'clock, Dedee was guided through several hallways before she got to the doorway through which she would walk when her name was called to receive the medal from the king. Her mother was escorted through the front door to sit with the guests. Four individuals were to receive medals, and she was informed she would be first.

When the king was in position, the crier called, "Madam Andrée de Jongh," and Dedee, dressed in a white two-piece wool suit, boldly walked out in front of the silent audience. When she reached a point six feet in front of the king, she turned to face him, curtsied, and stepped forward. The king, with members of HM Lifeguards in full, colorful regalia on both sides, wore a simple royal blue suit, and Dedee noticed his black, perfectly shined shoes.

The king seemed relaxed, and smiled at her. In a soft voice, inaudible to anyone in the audience, he said, "The highest of distinctions is in the service of others." He took the silver medal from a tray beside him and pinned it to her left lapel. "For the service you have rendered England, I thank you, as does our country and all its people."

Dedee was at a loss for words. He had a little trouble getting the clasp of the pin secured, and they both smiled.

"You have sacrificed much, mademoiselle, but always remember our gratitude."

He reached out with his right to shake hers, which Dedee had been told was the signal for her to leave, but he held on a bit longer, then put his left hand over hers with a slight bow of his head.

After saying, "Thank you, your majesty," Dedee took three steps backward, curtsied again, and walked out. From the corner of her eye, she saw her mother in the audience, beaming with pride.

The ceremony was over for Dedee, and she took a deep breath. She looked down at her medal. It was silver, with the likeness of King George wearing a crown, and hung from a purple ribbon. Her hands shook as she fingered the medal.

When all four recipients had been given their medals, the king took his leave, but the audience went to a large reception area, and after posing for photographs for the royal records, Dedee joined them. Dedee took another deep breath. This was the part she felt the least prepared for.

The first to greet her was Michael Cresswell, who hugged her and made a big fuss, telling her he had wanted them to trade

Himmler for her. They laughed, and Dedee surreptitiously surveyed the crowd, looking for Jack. She knew, if he was there, he would be taller than anyone else. No Jack.

Next came Elvire de Grief, and Dedee was elated to see her. Then Airey Neave and others from MI9. They talked about all the rescued fliers and all heaped praise on Dedee's bravery. Dedee looked around again, no Jack.

Her mother came up and put her arm around her. "Can you believe the king used both hands to shake yours?" she asked.

"Oh, Mom, that was nothing."

Dedee's mother watched her eyes with the understanding only a mother has. "He'll show up," she said. "Must be held up in traffic."

Elvire cornered her again. "We're pretty sure one of our 'packages' turned out to be an informant," she said. "He'll soon be arrested, and if I had my way, they'd hang him."

Dedee looked at her sharply, "No," she said. "Let it go. The war is over. I want us all to forget it."

Elvire saw the intensity in Dedee's eyes. "Of course, you are right," she said. "We've all had enough."

Dedee went out onto a balcony that overlooked the royal gardens. She thought about how the English had a special way with gardens. They were always so beautiful.

Then a voice. "Dedee! There you are."

She knew instantly who it was. Jack ran to her and enveloped her with his long arms, the same arms she had been dreaming of for two years. She returned the embrace and remembered how safe it had felt to be with him. It still did.

After a few moments, Jack held her away to look at her. "I cannot tell you how much I've wanted to thank you," he said. "You saved my life." His eyes started to tear up.

She looked up at him. "In so many ways, Jack, you saved mine, also."

Before her words could sink in, another woman walked up and put her arm around Jack.

Jack did likewise, and said, "This is my wife, Mary."

Dedee, taken aback, managed to say, "I've heard a lot about you." She saw that Mary was pregnant, and muttered weak congratulations, smiled, and excused herself.

She went to the other side of the portico, which looked out across the gardens toward Eaton Square. There, she saw her beloved black, yellow, and red Belgian flag waving in the gentle breeze, high above war-torn London. She thought of her father and wished he was still with her.

She realized her battle wasn't over. Many of her countrymen would still need help. She would find a way to give it.

END

To the Reader

The Postwoman is the story of Andrée (Dedee) de Jongh, a female Resistance fighter during World War II. Very little has been recorded of her exploits during that perilous time, and I wrote this book to shine a light on her life.

I've made every effort to create a historically accurate timeline. The interpretation of the characters is my own. As most files were destroyed before the Allies arrived, little or no documentation is available regarding specific details of Miss de Jongh's incarceration in Ravensbrück. As a result, many of her experiences detailed here are based on my interpretation and extensive research into similar WWII accounts.

At times, a choice needed to be made between conflicting historical recollections, and in these instances, the most logical course was chosen.

The incredible story of this brave young woman begged to be told, and for the liberties taken to share her story, I appreciate your understanding.

Michael Kenneth Smith

CREDITS

Peter Eisner. *The Freedom Line.* Harper Collins. 2013

Derek Shuff. *Evader.* The History Press. 2003

M.R.D. Foot and J.M. Langley. MI9: *Escape and Evasion.* Book Club Press. 1979

Sarah Helm. *Ravensbruck.* Anchor Books. 2013

Airey Neave. *Saturday at M.I.9.* Grafton 1979

John Nichol and Tony Rennell. *Home Run.* Viking. 2007

Sune Persson. *Escape from the Third Reich.* Skyhorse Publishing. 2010

Sherri Greene Otiss. *Silent Heros.* University Press of Kentucky. 2015

Airey Neave. *Little Cyclone.* Biteback Publishing. 2014

Judith Pearson. *The Wolves at the Door.* Lyons Press. 2008

Elizabeth Wein. *Rose Under Fire.* Disney-Hyperion. 2014

THE POSTWOMAN
EPILOGUE

❦

Andrée de Jongh: Dedee could not talk about the war and, specifically, the camps, for a long time after she was freed. She was quoted as saying, "For years after, whenever I felt the slightest bit gay, suddenly I would think of those that didn't make it, particularly my papa." When several of the fliers she had helped escape learned of her survival after the war, they sent her letters asking her to marry them. She never married. Some time after she had fully recovered, she trained as a nurse and worked in a leper colony in Ethiopia. She was held in such high esteem by the British, and particularly the RAF, that when her mother died, they sent a military plane to Ethiopia to transport her to the funeral, then returned her back. Years later, when she found out that a 'package' had talked, Dedee dismissed the matter, saying, "All is forgiven." The fact that she had changed her identity in Ravensbrück was not known until she mentioned it in a letter to Airey Neave in 1956.

Jack Newton: After the war Jack and his wife, Mary, settled down to raise their family. Dedee and Jack remained close exchanging letters and meeting every year at annual reunions of evaders and those that so bravely assisted them. Jack always referred to Dedee as his "second love."

Karl Gebhardt: As the coordinator of the surgical experiments at Ravensbrück and Auschwitz, Gebhardt was convicted of war crimes against humanity and sentenced to death. He was hanged in Landsberg Prison in Bavaria June 2, 1948.

Fritz Suhren: As the commandant of Ravensbrück, Suhren was tried, convicted and hanged in 1950. As the Russians were about to overtake Ravensbrück, Suhren took Odette Sansom, an inmate whom he believed was a niece of Winston Churchill and drove to the U.S. lines, hoping to get leniency. It didn't work.

Percival Treite: Became senior Ravensbrück doctor in December 1943. Charged with war crimes, he was sentenced to hang by a British Military Tribunal. Several surviving prisoners, however, wrote letters of support for the kindness Treite had exhibited. Notwithstanding, he committed suicide April 9, 1947.

Folke Bernadotte: Assisted in the liberation of nearly 31,000 prisoners held in German concentration camps. Following the war, Bernadotte was appointed by the UN as mediator in Palestine to assist in resolving the Palestinian/Israeli issues. He was assassinated by a Jewish terrorist group September 17, 1948.

Kurt Lischka: Imprisoned in France after the war, then extradited to Czechoslovakia in 1947 for war crimes there, but he was released in 1950. He lived in freedom for 25 years, then through efforts of holocaust survivors, he was arrested and sentenced to 10 years. He died May 16, 1989.

Florentino Goikoetxe: Hampered by the long-term effects of his leg wound, Florentino lived comfortably in his beloved Pyrenees and Basque country. He died July 27, 1980, and is buried near Ciboure.

Michael Cresswell: Continuing his diplomatic career after the war, Cresswell served in Greece, Iran, Finland, and Yugoslavia. He died in 1986 (age 77).

ACKNOWLEDGEMENTS

T hanks to my friend, Libby Jordan, who has acted as my media guru, support group, psychologist and an expert on everything having to do with books.

Thanks to Susannah Carlson who is my ruthless copy editor. She grinds up my text, spits it out and every time the manuscript gets better. Never an argument, but if we had one, she would win.

Thanks to Greg Michalson who has the patience of Jobe. His professionalism is unparalleled. His suggestions, particularly on structure have helped immensely.

Thanks to all my friends who have taken an interest in my writing. Your encouragement gets me back to my next project and keeps me going. You are the biggest reason I write.

Then there is my wife, Margie, who is always there through the ups and downs. The good reviews and the bad. She pulls me off the ceiling one day and picks me up off the floor the next. Without her...nothing.

Made in the USA
San Bernardino, CA
25 March 2019